Love and a Crocodile

Tanya Knight

TANYA KNIGHT

Contents

TANYA KNIGHT

About the Author

Dedication

Thank you to my readers who have made it as far as my
second novel.
This second book is a sequel to my debut, 'Men Are
Like Buses', but it's not essential to have read it.
I hope that you enjoy the shenanigans in the story.
Life is very short, so we just need to grab it by the horns
and run with it.
Make the most of every day.

Chapter 1

"What did you just say?" I asked incredulously of my friend, Evie. A buzzing sound started in my ears. I could feel my heart begin to race and my blood pressure rise. I felt a throb above my eyes. I really, really hoped that I had misheard her.

"I'm sorry," Evie stated. "I'm so very sorry. The last thing that I wanted was to hurt you. But I felt like you needed to know."

My heart sank. I looked around me blankly. There were forty or fifty people milling around. All guests of my own engagement party. Across the room I could see my fiancé, Jack. He was smiling at me. He had no idea that I had just been blindsided. We'd been together for a year. Last month Jack asked me to marry him. We'd gone away for the weekend to the Peak District. We'd climbed Kinder Scout, and at the top Jack had dropped to one knee and asked me to marry him.

I was ecstatic. Of course I had said yes. We'd been living together for well over six months, and everything had been going amazingly. Until today. Why, oh why did this have to happen?

I grabbed hold of Evie by her hand and pulled her outside with me. I needed a little space from my family and friends to try to understand what was going on.

"What do you mean? In what way are you seeing Jack? I'm confused," I asked.

"I'm really sorry Lily," replied Evie. "We've been having an affair for quite a few months now. I tried to fight it, but I just couldn't help myself. I'm so sorry to have hurt you like this."

I couldn't believe what I was hearing. How was it even possible that Jack was having an affair? And with Evie, one of my closest friends? I felt physically sick at the thought of it.

"How did it start? When do you see each other?" I asked.

"He started messaging me a long time ago – actually from the very first time I met him, which was on your thirtieth birthday last year. I tried to stay away from him but I can't help myself. I'm in love with him Lily."

I was devastated. How could Evie be in love with Jack? He's my boyfriend. Well, he's my fiancé actually. How can this be? I suddenly realised that I was going to be sick. I ran over to some bushes and tasted that horrible bile that you get initially. I was soon coughing and spluttering the sick from my mouth.

My head pounded. I walked back towards Evie and sank to the floor, leaning my back against the bricks of the hall, the venue for my engagement party. I felt like my world was crumbling around me.

"How often do you see him?" I asked.

"A couple of times a week usually. Sometimes he comes to my house or we've met up in a hotel a few times. A few months back we stopped seeing each other, but we couldn't keep it up. I felt so lonely, I couldn't help but message him and start things up again," said Evie.

"You make me sick," I raged. "How could you do this to me? How could he do this to me? I thought he was the one. I thought he was my forever person."

I sobbed. My emotions were all over the place. I had switched from angry to debilitatingly sad in the space of a second.

"Please go. I can't even bear to look at you."

I shook my head at Evie. She sighed. She stepped backwards and walked away mumbling her apologies. She headed to her car and moments later drove out of the car park.

The door to the community hall opened.

"Lily," called my best friend Molly. "What are you doing out here? People are wondering where you are?"

Molly and I had been best friends since the day we started secondary school together. We instantly gravitated towards each other that very first morning, and she'd been by my side pretty much the rest of my life.

Molly stepped in front, looking quizzically down at me.

"Have you been crying?" she asked. "What's happened? And was that Evie just driving off?"

Molly sat down next to me, put her arms around me and gave me a hug. I always felt better when Molly was around. She's like a ray of sunshine. I sobbed into her shoulder and explained what had happened.

"That's not possible. Jack loves you. I just don't believe it," Molly exclaimed.

Suddenly I felt hope. Maybe Molly was right. Maybe Evie, for some bizarre reason, had made the whole thing up. Maybe she had developed some infatuation for Jack, and Jack had no part in it. Dare I believe that's the case?

"We need to talk to Jack," stated Molly. "Find out what's truly going on. I'll go and find him. Last time I saw him he was talking to Harry. Are you alright to wait here a moment?"

I nodded my assent and watched as Molly headed back into the hall. I took a deep, steadying breath. I needed to keep my wits about me. Maybe all was not lost after all. Harry is Molly's boyfriend. They've been together just a few weeks longer than Jack and me. The four of us are firm friends and we hang out together the majority of the time.

The door opens again, and Molly reappears with Jack and also Harry in tow.

"What's going on?" asked Jack. "Why do I need to come outside?"

Jack looked very confused when he saw me sitting on the floor. I scrambled up and looked him square in the eye.

"You tell me, Jack" I replied. "What is going on? I've just had a very enlightening conversation with Evie."

Jack fidgeted. He looked at the floor. He wouldn't look me in the eye. He looked truly shifty.

"What? What conversation have you had?" asked Jack.

"Evie has been telling me about your affair." I spat out the words. "What the fuck Jack? How could you do this to me? I thought we were happy?"

"Oh fuck," said Jack. "I was trying to end it. I don't know how I got myself into this situation."

"Evie said that you started messaging her after my birthday last year. That's nearly a whole year ago! You've seriously been seeing my friend for months behind my back?"

"Well, that's not quite true," replied Jack. "For many months we were just sending messages back and forth. It's only been the last few months that we've been meeting up."

"But why?" I asked. "I thought our relationship was great? Our sex life is amazing. We were going to get married. I loved you. Why would you ask me to marry you when all this time you are shagging Evie behind my back?"

It just didn't make sense. I couldn't compute this story with my happy ending. I truly felt like the bottom had fallen out of my world. I needed to understand. I needed to know what I did wrong.

"What did I do wrong, Jack?" I asked sadly.

"It's not you Lily," said Jack. "It's me".

Wow. With those words I switched again from sad to angry.

"You realise that's the biggest cliché in the world? Of course it's not me. You are the fucking idiot here. You just wanted whatever you wanted with no thought for the consequences. You are an absolute tosser. I can't believe that I am in love with someone as selfish as you."

I was angry. I was hurt. I was lashing out. I don't normally swear, but I just wanted to shout, to scream and to call him the 'C' word. But I was woefully aware that my parents and friends were all just a few feet away. No doubt wondering where I had gone. Little did they know that my entire world had just imploded.

"I'm going home," I decided. "You can tell everyone whatever you like, but I can't go back in there. And I can't face any questions. Molly, can you come home with me please? And Jack. Don't even think about coming back. You are not welcome. You can come and pick up some clothes tomorrow, but for now, I can't face seeing you."

With that, I turned around and walked towards Molly's car. She unlocked the doors and I sat in the passenger seat, with tears pouring down my face.

Twenty minutes later I collapsed onto my sofa. Molly headed into the kitchen and switched the kettle on.

"Tea or wine?" she asked.

"Well, that's a silly question," I replied.

Molly switched the kettle off and turned to the fridge instead. She pulled out a bottle of Sauvignon Blanc and reached for two glasses from the cupboard.

"How are you feeling?" Molly asked.

"Devastated," I responded. "Gutted, broken, unbelieving and truly horrified. What the hell am I going to do?"

"Well, first we are going to talk," replied Molly. "Then you are going to get angry, then you are going to get sad. Then you are going to be brave. But one step at a time. I'm here for you Lily. Always have been and always will be. Jack is an absolute imbecile. He's thrown everything away. What an absolute twat."

"I'm so disappointed Molly," I said. "I love him so much. I just can't believe it".

"I can't believe that Evie did this to you either," said Molly. "What was she thinking? The whole world knew what a great couple you and Jack were."

I truly couldn't understand why Jack had done this to me. I had no idea that there was anything wrong in our relationship. I had been blissfully happy. I was so excited to get engaged. I had the whole rest of my life mapped out, and Jack was always by my side. He was my person.

Molly and I spent the rest of the evening drinking vast quantities of wine and talking through things. I'd had a number of text messages and calls on my phone from family and friends, so I just turned it off. I couldn't deal with anyone else right now. Molly messaged my parents to let them know that I was ok and just needed a bit of time and space to process things. Apparently Jack had left the hall straight after we did, so all the guests were extremely bemused by what was happening. Still, that was the least of my worries right now.

Thank goodness for Molly. She really was the best friend. She allowed me to fall apart, and she just held the pieces in place until I was ready to pick things up again. Grief is a process. And finding out that your fiancé has been having an affair for months is truly devastating and would take some time to work through. The hardest part was giving up on the dreams. I had built Jack up and placed him on such a pedestal. It was awful realising that actually he was weak, thoughtless and selfish. Giving up my dreams of happy ever after with Jack was so hard. I felt like I had climbed the stairs of life, got to the top step, was just about to step over the finish line and then I slid all the way to the bottom again.

Chapter 2

Two months later and I was finally starting to feel together again. The year had progressed, spring had turned into summer, and my world was finally brightening up. I still felt incredibly sad when I thought about Jack, but some things were great again. During the first couple of weeks following our split, we gave notice on our house and I moved in with Molly. Originally this was going to be a temporary measure, but I was still here. And Molly was happy with the arrangements. Her and Harry continued to have separate houses despite spending most nights together. Harry still lived with his friend James, and they were only a few streets away, so it was a convenient arrangement.

James and I had dated once, but then he'd finished with me to rekindle his relationship with a girl called Jasmine. We'd remained good friends ever since. Needless to say, things hadn't worked out for James and Jasmine, and they had split up a few weeks after Jack and I got together. James was currently dating a girl called Nat and they'd been together for about six months.

I was finding it quite hard being single again. I'd had no contact with either Jack or Evie for weeks now. Other than handing over Jack's possessions, I wanted nothing further to do with him. He'd broken my heart and there was no way back from that. He had suggested trying to move forwards as a couple, but there was no way that I could forgive him. He'd even suggested going to couples counselling, but I'm just not that sort of person. He'd broken my trust as well as my heart, and I didn't want to be one of those people constantly worrying and checking up on my partner. I needed to feel that trust, yet I doubted it could be truly restored. Maybe forgiveness would work for some people, but it wouldn't work for me.

I'd decided that I was better off alone, at least for the moment. I needed to rebuild my life and find my mojo again. Molly and Harry had gone away this weekend and I was feeling at a bit of a loose end. I decided that I'd head out for a run. I'd only started running at the start of last year, but I'd really enjoyed it, and was now a regular parkrunner. I had completed my first half marathon last September and had been delighted with that milestone.

As I set out on my run, I thought back to the half marathon race. It had been a hot day, and the course was winding through a forest and around a lake. I'd had a good build up to the run, and Jack had come along to support me. It was an amazingly beautiful venue in a National Trust estate and I had spotted about thirty roe deer and a couple of muntjac. I had crossed the finish line in a time of 2 hours and 12 minutes and had been delighted with that effort. It was the furthest distance I had ever run. I was so happy to receive my first medal, and proudly hung it on the wall. I hoped to create a medal collection with some more races this summer. Jack had been so proud of me and we had an amazing evening out celebrating.

That's what I miss most about being in a relationship. It's having someone to share the adventures with. I'm so lucky to have Molly, she has truly been a godsend.

Today, I was running through the park and heading down to an area that I called Bluebell wood. It was actually James that had initially showed me that route, and I fondly recall running it with him for the first time. Alongside Bluebell wood is a river bank which is popular with dogs and cyclists. I decided to head along the river and see where I ended up.

A short way along there was a jetty, and a group of ladies were chatting and getting changed. I stopped to watch them wondering if they were going swimming. Although it was early summer, the river temperature is still low, so I thought they were very brave.

"Good morning," called out one of the ladies. "Beautiful day isn't it?"

"Morning," I replied. "It is gorgeous today. Are you going in for a swim?"

"Yes," she replied. "Want to join us?"

"I'd love to one day, but not today." I said.

"My name is Rachel and I swim here most days, so you'd be welcome to join me whenever you wish."

"Hi Rachel, I'm Lily. That sounds fabulous. Do you swim at the same time every day?"

"No," replied Rachel. "Are you on Facebook? If you join the Castledyke Bluetits group, everyone posts up the swim times, and you're welcome to join any of the groups."

"That sounds fabulous," I replied. "I will do that. I love the name Bluetits."

"It's quite appropriate," laughed Rachel. "The Bluetits is a worldwide swimming organisation for those interested in open water swimming in rivers and lakes. We are just the local branch of the Bluetits group."

"That's fascinating," I replied. "I'd love to join you. I will certainly look you up on Facebook and then meet up with you. Are you swimming tomorrow by any chance?"

"Yes, definitely. I will be swimming with most of these ladies tomorrow at 10am. Would you like to join us then?"

"That sounds perfect. I will see you then. What do I need to bring?"

"You just need to wear your swimming costume. Some of us use neoprene gloves and boots although the water isn't too cold this time of year. It's about 15 degrees currently. I can lend you some boots and a tow float for your first swim. Just make sure that you bring warm clothes to change into afterwards. Some choose to wear a swim cap and goggles, but most of us just swim breaststroke so don't need them. There's no pressure. It's just fun and relaxed. A hot drink in a flask is a good idea, and a towel of course."

"You are so kind," I said. "I'll look forward to seeing you tomorrow."

"Enjoy the rest of your run," replied Rachel.

I continue running along the river bank smiling to myself. I feel like this is a step in the right direction. The ladies looked really nice, were having a great chat and clearly were very welcoming and friendly. It's so nice when you meet new people and get to know them. I was looking forward to having my first dip tomorrow.

Later, having completed my run, showered and sat down, I searched and joined the Castledyke Bluetits page. It was a busy page, and a quick scroll through showed lots of groups of people posting about various swims throughout the day. It looked like there would be plenty of opportunities to get in the river.

The first swim of the day was at 6:30 a.m. by a group called 'The Early Crew'. That was definitely a bit too early for me. I was surprised to see that they swim all year round at that time. It must be pitch black and freezing cold in the winter months.

The next group seemed to swim around 7:30 a.m. and they call themselves the NSEC. It took me a while to find out what that acronym stood for, but eventually saw that they are the 'Not So Early Crew.' I laughed out loud when I figured that out.

The other regular swim of the day was a group called the CBA group. That one stumped me. I couldn't see what that stood for and made a mental note to ask Rachel tomorrow.

The next morning it was rather drizzly. I wasn't sure if the Bluetits would still be swimming, so I messaged the Facebook page to ask. I had a swift reply informing me that the swims generally do go ahead even if it's raining. It seems the only time that they don't go ahead are when it would be dangerous to swim. Apparently, that's usually if there has been very heavy rain or if some specific type of algae develops on the river.

I gathered up my belongings, packed a bag and made a flask of tea. I knew that I was likely to be very cold after my swim so I wanted to be prepared. At 10 a.m. I was standing by the side of the jetty chatting to Rachel.

"How long have you been wild swimming?" I asked.

"About five years now. I try to swim every day," said Rachel.

"Wow, that's dedication," I replied.

"It keeps me sane," laughed Rachel. "I'm a paramedic, so wild swimming helps me to deal with the pressure of the job. I used to be a runner, but replaced that with wild swimming. It's really good for your mental health and places less stress on your body."

We continued chatting. I remembered to ask Rachel about the CBA group. That apparently stands for 'Can't Be Arsed' as they usually meet later in the day than the earlier groups. That gave me a proper laugh out loud moment.

By this time, everyone was changed and ready to get in the river. Rachel had kindly lent me a bright pink tow float and some neoprene socks.

"The tow float is really for other river users to see you," explained Rachel. "If you are rowing or in a boat, it's important that the swimmers are highly visible, and fluorescent tow floats and swim hats are the best way to achieve that. Of course, it's also handy as a safety aid, should you get into difficulty."

Rachel went on to advise me never to swim on my own. You should always have someone with you should you need assistance.

Whilst we were talking, the other ladies were getting in the river. There were a lot of oohs, and aahs, and quite a few swear words as well. And then it was my turn.

I turned around and stepped onto the ladder, lowering myself into the water. I'm a competent swimmer so have no concerns about that, but my god it was cold! I felt my breath catch in my throat.

"Concentrate on breathing out slowly," advised Rachel. "That will help you relax, and then you will be able to catch your breath."

I concentrated hard on doing exactly that, and in a few seconds I was able to breath normally.

"I can't believe how the cold water took my breath away," I exclaimed to Rachel.

"It gets easier with practice," she replied. "Even in the summer time it's still very cold if you aren't conditioned to it. We are going to swim to that tree over there," she said, pointing to a tree a few hundred metres away.

Off we go and I'm swimming along with the rest of the ladies. I've relaxed now and my body seems to have acclimatised to the water. A feeling of tranquillity and contentment washes over me. I look upstream and see a mummy duck with five ducklings, whilst downstream are two swans gazing intently at us. I feel like I'm connecting with nature, and it's an unfamiliar but very good feeling.

As we swim along I get introduced to the other ladies. The names flow over my head, but I smile and say hi to them all. There was a Chloe, a Sarah, a Lyn and a Gail. They all had beaming smiles and were very welcoming. Various topics of conversation took place around me. Talk of the weather, the swimming, a forthcoming trip to the coast, and a visit to the pub for lunch. They kindly invite me to join them, and as I'm at a loose end today, I gladly accepted.

After about half an hour, we had swum to the tree and returned to the jetty. The return swim leg was significantly quicker than the outward one as we were then swimming with the current rather than against it. As I climbed out of the water, I noticed that my legs and arms were all bright red from the cold. I looked like I'd got sunburn.

Rachel advised me to get dressed as quickly as possible, so the next few minutes were spent doing just that. It's quite hard to put clothes on when your hands are numb, so I made a mental note to wear easier clothes next time. Most of the ladies have a dry robe which is like a cross between a big dressing gown and a coat. They are able to get changed underneath the dry robe, so gaining a little more privacy. Of course, anyone could be walking past watching us get changed.

After the swim, we gathered together for a photograph which one of the ladies posted onto the Bluetit page on Facebook. My watch tells me that I swam for 750m and took about 25 minutes. I'm happy with that for my first attempt. We then headed off to the pub where we had a most enjoyable hour eating, chatting and laughing. They really are a very interesting and fun bunch of ladies – from all different walks of life. But all sharing the love of wild swimming. I feel very grateful to have bumped into them this weekend and I'm excited for my future swims.

Chapter 3

On Sunday night Molly arrived home from her weekend away with Harry. She's happy, smiling and seems very relaxed.

"How are you Lily? Did you manage to keep busy over the weekend?"

I filled Molly in on my Bluetit adventures. She listened intently while I tried to describe the feeling of contentment and serenity that I experienced.

"Rather you than me. I'm not a fan of cold water," Molly commented. "How nice that you went to lunch afterwards. Did you feel comfortable with the ladies? Do you think they will become friends over time?"

"Definitely," I answered. "They were so welcoming and nice. It was interesting because they all had different jobs and lifestyles, were different ages and levels of fitness, yet were all bound by the love of wild swimming. They did all seem slightly bonkers mind, but I guess that's a bit of a prerequisite for that kind of hobby."

"Well, much as I love you Lils, you won't catch me joining you for regular cold swims, that's for sure," laughed Molly. It's well known that Molly is not a fan of anything cold, energetic or that requires trainers or a tent. It's amazing that we are such close friends really when we are such different people. I love a challenge, enjoy adventures and like to stay fit. Molly prefers to dress up in nice clothes and makeup, stay in hotels and stay warm and dry.

This weekend had been really good for me. With recent events, I have struggled a little mentally, and it's taken me some time to get back my normal positive attitude. But now I feel like it's time to move onwards and upwards. Make new friends, get back to doing some fun activities and maybe I'll even think about dating again.

On that note, Molly has suggested a couple of times that I sign up to a dating site. It's not something I've done before. I'm more of a face-to-face kind of person rather than a messaging girl really, but equally I guess it would give me access to a broader pool of potential dates. It might be worth a try anyway.

"How about we spend the evening together with a bottle of wine, and we sign me up to a dating site," I suggested. "Just as an experiment….." I added quickly.

"That's a great idea," replied Molly. "It will be fun."

An hour later we had settled with a glass of wine each and an ice bucket for the rest of the bottle. We had another bottle lined up in the fridge (just in case).

We spent the first few minutes discussing which dating site we should go for. There are quite a few out there, some larger than others. Tinder is probably the biggest one, then there is Bumble which seems quite popular. I swayed towards a site called 'Just Date' which promised a really simple, easy dating site which didn't cost too much.

"Just Date it is then," stated Molly. "Now to find a profile picture of you."

We had been flicking through my Facebook profile trying to find the nicest pictures. In view of the fact that I like men who are sporty and busy, we had collected together a few pictures from the past few years. There was one of me swimming, one on a bike and one with a glass of wine. The most flattering picture was when I had borrowed one of Molly's dresses, so we decided that should be my profile pic.

"That's a good selection," said Molly. "The dress picture shows off your sophisticated side, and the other action pictures show off your sporty side. I think that's the perfect combination."

"I have a sophisticated side?" I laughed.

"Of course you do," responded Molly. "You are naturally beautiful and well spoken. You don't need to be posh or wear lots of makeup to be sophisticated you know."

Molly really is a sweetheart, and great at boosting one's self-esteem.

We spent the new few minutes putting together the bio. I made sure to emphasize that I am a sporty girl, and I'm looking for a guy to have some adventures with. A few more clicks, a quick flash of the debit card, and my profile is ready to go live. Now we just have to see if we get any responses.

Well, that was the first bottle of wine polished off nicely. Clearly, we needed to open the second one. Molly went and grabbed it out of the fridge and popped it in the ice bucket.

"I'm not really convinced about the online dating thing," I confessed to Molly. "I've only signed up for a week initially."

"That will give you a chance to see what it's like," agreed Molly. "And then you can either renew or sack it off at the end of the week. It will be interesting to see what type of guys contact you."

By the time I'm halfway down my glass of wine I've received a notification that my profile is now live. Over the next ten minutes I can see that I've collected a bunch of 'likes' and a couple of guys have messaged me already. The app has a page putting together all those that have liked you. I have the chance to swipe right if I like them back, or swipe left to dismiss them. There is another page of messages for those that have actually taken the time to write to me.

I check out the two guys that have messaged me already. One is nearly fifty and looks old enough to be my dad. And the other one is nineteen. That's just way too young.

"There must be a way to set the parameters of the guys that get to see you on the app," suggested Molly.

I head into the app settings and indeed there is. I set my boundaries at twenty-five and forty. I really don't want to go younger or older than that.

There is also a section with 'starter questions' that you can send to people that you like the look of. They seem to be really random, so I dismiss using those – at this stage at least.

I clicked on the page of people that have liked my profile. The ones that are just a non-starter get swiftly swiped away. There are a couple of interesting looking ones, so I drilled down to read their bios before deciding what to do. One is thirty-three, Marc, and he is a keen ultra runner. He looks cute. He has a cheeky smile on his primary photo. And he looks fit and lean. I liked the fact that he runs, and he only lives about twelve miles away – so that is definitely a possibility.

"What do you think to this one Molly?" I asked, showing her the profile.

"Interesting," she replied. "He is good looking. He shares your interests and he's fairly local. Sounds ideal to me. Why don't you message him?"

Whilst I'm deliberating that option, I have already swiped right to indicate that I'm liking the look of him. I can see that he's online and while I'm figuring out what to write, a message pops over from him. Well, that saved me from having to make the first move.

I like your bio. You sound really fun and you are very pretty in your pictures too. I love the fact that you run too. Do you belong to a running club or do you run on your own or with friends?

That's quite a good message to send initially. It's flattering and complimentary whilst also asking a direct question. I'm already typing out a message back to him.

I'm not a member of a running club yet but it is something that I've thought about. I need to look into it. I have seen some running tops for 'Castledyke Runners' at parkrun so was considering talking to them initially. I usually run on my own but I do have a few friends that I run with occasionally.

I can see that Marc was already replying to my message.

A couple of my friends run with Castledyke Runners. I've been told it's a warm and welcoming club. I tend to train on my own as I run quite long distances and it puts most people off running with me. But luckily I'm happy in my own company so it's not too much of an issue. Would you like to meet up with me for an easy run this week? We could just go for a relaxing 10km?

I showed the response to Molly. She told me to accept his invitation. She thinks I should join him for a run and see how we get on.

He does sound nice, so I decide to go for it. I messaged Marc back and arranged to meet him Tuesday evening at a park in Castledyke for a run. It's midway between us, so seems like a sensible meeting point.

Well that all happened rather quickly. I'm pleased that I took the initiative to sign up after all. Maybe it wouldn't be a waste of time and money.

The rest of the evening passed quickly. I swapped numbers with Marc, and gathered a number of other likes on my profile. A few other men messaged me but none that I was really interested in. I felt bad not replying to them, but it seemed almost kinder than responding with a 'No thanks'.

Tuesday evening came round swiftly. I was rooting through my drawers looking for my favourite running kit to wear for my run with Marc. It's quite hard to make a good impression in Lycra unless you have the most amazing physique of course. I like to think that I look ok, but I'm hardly a supermodel. At 5ft6 I'm just over average height, but I have a long body and short legs. That's the opposite to most supermodels who seem to have obscenely long legs.

A short while later I parked up just a couple of minutes from where I had arranged to meet Marc. I jumped out, locked the car, zipped my car key into a pocket in the back of my leggings and hurried across to the designated meeting point.

As I approached the spot, I see that Marc was already there. I was pleasantly surprised that he did actually look just like his photo. I'm not sure what I expected, but I wouldn't have been surprised if it had been someone completely different.

"Hello Lily," smiled Marc. "How are you? It's lovely to meet you. You look very nice."

"I'm good thanks," I responded. "I'm pleased to see that you look just like your photo. I was slightly nervous that you might have used someone else's photo."

"I know what you mean," said Marc. "I've only met one other lady from 'Just Date' and she was a bit of a surprise. She had obviously used a photo for her profile that was many years old so I was a bit disappointed when we met up in person. We'd been chatting for about three weeks so there was a fair bit of build-up. There was unfortunately no attraction whatsoever when we met, from my side in any case."

"I'm surprised it didn't put you off the app," I queried.

"Well, it did a little bit, but I signed up for a month so I thought I might as well make the most of my investment," he said.

We discussed the route that he had planned for us to run. It sounded really nice. I had never run in this park before so I was happy to let him guide me. We started off steadily around the perimeter of the park and then along a neighbouring river bank. There weren't any swimmers in the river, but we did see lots of swans and some people rowing. Marc explained that there was a rowing club headquarters just a couple of miles away and therefore it was very common to see people rowing here.

We spent the next few kilometres chatting companionably. Marc seemed like a really nice guy. Well informed about many subjects. We touched on jobs, local and central politics and of course running. I asked Marc about what type of events he ran in, and he told me about some of the previous events he has competed in. He has done a few 24 hour races where you run a circuit as many times as you can in 24 hours. Marc managed to complete over 108 miles which is pretty awesome. He's also completed Race to the Stones which is a 100km race from the Chiltern Hills to the Avebury Stone Circle in Wiltshire. Last year he competed in a Backyard Ultra. That seems like a crazy event. You have to run just over 4 miles every hour on the hour. That sounds quite achievable to me, until I realise that it's a last man standing event and that the winner was running for over 3 and a half days. Marc managed two days which is pretty amazing. I just can't quite get my head around taking on a challenge like that. I was impressed at completing my half marathon but that seems like nothing compared to the distances that Marc likes to run.

I was pleased that we didn't get onto the subject of past relationships. I'm not ready to talk about mine yet so I was glad that the conversation stayed elsewhere. In what felt like no time at all we had completed our 10km run and returned to the original meeting point.

Having not ever met anyone for a 'run-date' before I wasn't quite sure of the etiquette. Would we kiss? Did I want him to kiss me? Whilst I was attracted to him, I was also breathing quite heavily and was rather sweaty. I wasn't sure that kissing me right now would be the most pleasant experience for him. I was therefore quite relieved when he didn't try. He gave me a very brief hug and a quick peck on the cheek when it was time to say goodbye. We hadn't arranged to meet up again, so I wasn't quite sure if he had enjoyed himself. We seemed to get on well enough but being rather inexperienced at these things, I found it hard to gauge his level of interest. On the drive home I pondered if I wanted to see him again. I think so. Certainly if he reached out to me I would be happy to meet him again. But I wasn't sure that I would be the one to make the first move. I guess I will just wait and see if he contacts me.

Upon arriving home I briefed Molly on the details of the date. She was surprised that we hadn't arranged to meet again but was happy that things had gone to plan. She thought he was probably just playing it a little cool and would be in touch in due course. I said that I would just go with the flow and see what happened.

By the next evening I hadn't heard anything from Marc. I was a little surprised to find that I was actually a bit disappointed in this. I imagine it's more from my confidence taking a bit of a knocking than because I really was attracted to Marc. But, he did seem nice and we chatted easily together. I did enjoy running with him.

Thursday night however he was back in touch. It turned out that he'd been away for work (he is an Architect) and had a full line up of meetings and dinner out with clients, so hadn't had a chance to reach out to me. I was pleased to hear from him and readily agreed to meeting up with him on Saturday. He suggested a picnic this time and I liked the sound of that. I had a busy day planned for Saturday now as I was planning on going to parkrun first thing, then I was meeting up with some Bluetits for a swim and then meeting Marc for a picnic in the afternoon. That's exactly my perfect sort of day so I was looking forward to it.

Molly asked if I would renew my 'Just Date' membership after the first week and I wasn't planning on it. There had been loads of likes from people, but it was really only Marc that had piqued my interest. I am definitely only interested in getting to know one person at a time, so would allow the membership to lapse. I always had the option of renewing it again in the future if I chose to. I'd see if things progressed with Marc before considering dating online again.

Chapter 4

Saturday morning was overcast and dry, ideal weather for parkrun. I'd decided that it would be a good day to have a crack at improving my PB (personal best). I had managed to do this on a number of occasions over the past year, but the target was getting pretty hard now. The target time to beat is 24:43.

I arrived about 8:45 a.m. and made sure to keep moving around so that I didn't get chilly or stiffen up. I was happy to see that James had arrived, so I went over to say hi. James hadn't been to parkrun for a few months, so it was good to see him again. In fact, I hadn't been to parkrun for a while either. I'd got out of the habit of doing it after splitting up with Jack. But now that I was focusing on rebuilding my life, I found that my enthusiasm and motivation had returned.

"Lily, hi! How are you? You are looking well," said James.

"Thanks James, it's good to see you. It's been a while since we last met," I replied.

"Indeed it has. Not for at least three or four months I would think." James lowered his voice. "I was sorry to hear that you split up from Jack. How are you feeling about everything now?"

"I'm good thanks. It's taken a little time to be fair. I was pretty devastated but I'm feeling much better now. It's time to move forwards and grab life by the horns," I replied.

"That's great to hear. I'm pleased you're back on the up. You've always been a happy and positive person, so I had no doubt you would bounce back in time," said James.

It was time to gather around for the briefing from the Run Director. We listened to the details and then headed to the start line. 3,2,1 parkrun……

I'd started fairly near the front so it was the customary flying start. Things would settle down after a few hundred metres, but the runners surged forwards like a wave. I'd lost James in the melee but would most likely find him at the end. I was more comfortable running alone as I often felt guilty that I'd be slowing James down if he ran with me.

After we'd dated a couple of years back, we had always had a good friendship. It felt good to see James, and I was happy that I'd bumped into him again.

By the end of the first lap my lungs were starting to burn. I'd pushed harder than normal and was certainly feeling the difference. I knew that, later on towards the end, my legs would start to tire as well but it was currently just the lungs.

By the end of the second lap that little voice in my head was shouting loud and clear.

Just slow down.

You don't need to run this fast.

It's not your day today.

No-one cares what your time is anyway so why not just take it easier?

I always found that the voice inside your head gets louder the longer you run. Previous experiences educate you how to ignore that voice, or even better, replace it with positive mantras.

You've got this.

You are nearly there. Just keep the pace you are going.

You're going to feel so happy when you fly over the finish line knowing that you've given it 100%.

It's common knowledge that parkrun is not designed to be a race, but an inclusive community of people enjoying running and walking together. However, there is definitely a competitive element for some people. There are many who love looking at their statistics, analysing their performances and comparing themselves to others. Equally, parkrun is just as important to those walking 5km for the first time. There are mental and physical health benefits to completing parkrun on a regular basis for everyone regardless of their speed, age and fitness levels. Certainly, I felt that I had become part of a community of people who enjoy meeting up each Saturday morning and I have achieved considerable mental and physical benefits from attending regularly.

Right now however, I felt PAIN. I was heading down the straight to the finish funnel and a quick glance at my Garmin reassured me that I was on track for a PB. I was currently on 24:15 and there were only a few more metres to run. I flew over the finish line around 24:22 and was delighted to slow down to a walk. I held out my hand for my finish token, and smiled appreciation at the high-viz clad volunteer who handed it to me.

I moved over towards a tree as my legs were struggling to support me. James came over having clearly finished sometime before as he wasn't even breathing heavily.

"Wow Lily. You were awesome. I thought you'd be another couple of minutes before you finished. You must be delighted," James said.

"Very, happy," I puffed. I could only speak one word at a time. I really had put 100% into that run. And I was so pleased. That was a new PB for sure.

"Have you got time to go for a coffee?" James asked.

"Unfortunately, I don't I'm afraid. I'm meeting some new friends for a swim in the river shortly," I replied.

"Wow," said James. "That sounds fun. Have you been doing river swimming long?"

"No, not really. In fact, this will be my second time swimming with this group," I responded. "But they seem really nice, and I'm enjoying getting to know them."

"I'm so glad that you are getting out and about again," said James. "I was hoping you would be here today as I wanted to make sure you were ok."

I felt a warm glow build up inside me. It was nice to know that James still cared. At one time we had been really into each other, but then he'd finished with me to rekindle things with Jasmine. I wasn't sure if that door could ever be reopened, and I was fairly sure he was settled with a different girlfriend now in any case.

"Well it was great to see you James. I will hope to see you again soon. I am up for a coffee sometime, but just not today."

"Perfect," replied James. "I will send you a message during the week and we can arrange a meet up."

"Spot on. Enjoy your weekend," I said as I turned away and started walking towards the exit of the park.

An hour later, I was once again standing on the jetty chatting to Rachel and Gail. I had on some slightly more suitable clothes today which should make getting changed after the swim a bit easier. I had a pair of tracksuit trousers with zips down the outside of the legs which would make getting them on much less troublesome than last time.

I'd been telling the ladies about my running date with Marc during the week. It seemed I was alone in thinking that a 10km run is a good first date. They were much more keen on the picnic concept that we had for our second date. I was looking forward to meeting up with Marc later today. He'd messaged me a couple of times, so we'd arranged to meet up at Castledyke where he knew of a lovely picnic area beside the river, about a mile or so upstream from where we met last time.

There were a few more swimmers for me to meet today. There was another Rachel, a Sara and a Beth. Today the Bluetits were telling me about a series of challenges that they regularly undertook. These generally encouraged swimming on a regular basis throughout the year, covering either a minimum amount of time or distance each month. Some of them were aiming for 10,000 metres this month, and Beth was aiming for 25,000 metres during the month. Wow. That seemed like a serious amount of swimming to me. I was happy with my 750 metres for the moment.

Our conversation then turned to what might be lurking in the water. There were many answers, and much laughter, to my questions about what I might bump into in the water.

"Well," said Beth. "Further downstream, near town, you might bump into a shopping cart or two. But around here the only non-living things you are likely to bump into are logs, sticks and weed in the summer months. Occasionally you might find some rubbish that's been dumped, or even in the summer months, you might find that one of the boats have emptied their toilet. They aren't supposed to do it, but it does happen infrequently."

"Yes, that's pretty minging," said Rachel. "But it's thankfully quite rare. We do however get a lot of fish. Most of them are small, but there are some pretty sizeable pike in here, and you occasionally might feel them bump into you."

"That's right," agreed Sara. "I always get scared when my tow float bumps into me. I often think it's a fish, then just realise the wind has picked up and it's my own tow float."

"And of course there is the seal," stated Rachel.

"Seal," I exclaimed. "There's a seal?"

"Yes, there is," replied Rachel. "There is a seal that's been living in the river for about two years. It's never bothered the Bluetit swimmers though. It's quite shy. It occasionally comes out to play with the paddleboarders in the summer, but it tends to stay away from groups of swimmers."

"I'd love to see a seal in the river," I stated. "Although I think I'd be quite scared if it tried to swim next to me. They can have quite a vicious bite I believe."

"They do indeed," replied Rachel. "One of my friends used to work at a seal sanctuary, and she told me that a seal's bite is stronger than that of an Alsatian."

"I think I'd be swimming as quickly as possible in the other direction," I laughed.

We queued up along the jetty, sliding one by one into the water. Those already in then struck out towards the turnaround tree. As I entered the water, I once again experienced that 'take your breath away' moment, but this time consciously thought about slowly exhaling through my mouth preventing any panic or hyperventilation. I felt quite proud of myself, especially as the lady behind me was swimming for the first time, so I even felt able to offer her the same advice too.

The laughing and chatting between the Bluetits was wonderful to hear. I experienced that lovely feeling of tranquillity once again. I didn't see any ducks this time, but we did get a glimpse of an otter. What a wonderful sight to see. The otter struck out from the far bank, swam towards us and disappeared underneath the jetty. Apparently, he can often be found on a ledge underneath the jetty.

As we approached the turn-around tree, some of the ladies were discussing swimming a little further. I decided to stick with them as I was very comfortable today, and not even really feeling the cold yet. We swam for an extra few minutes and then turned around. This time on the way back I used the goggles that I had brought and swam some front crawl. It took a lot more energy and it was quite disconcerting putting my head under the water. The water was murky and dark lower down but the visibility near the surface was surprisingly good. I wasn't able to see any fish which might have been a good thing. I had spotted a few small fish when I was stood on the jetty earlier. Thankfully, there was no sign of any seals today.

In what felt like no time at all, I was clambering up the steps of the ladder onto the jetty. My skin had turned red again, and felt extremely cold to the touch, but I didn't feel too cold in myself. I was looking forward to being back in dry, warm clothes. Getting changed was much more pleasurable today and I was soon sipping my cup of tea. I'd popped a warm hat and gloves on, although I was soon able to take them off as the sun came out and I could feel the heat gradually warming me.

Once everyone had changed, we gathered on the wall at the bottom of the tow path to enable one of the Bluetits to setup a camera to take a picture of us all. This would be posted onto the Facebook group. The ladies started to organise when they would be swimming next, so I decided to head home to get showered. I was still due to nip to the supermarket to pick up some supplies for our picnic. Marc had said that he was providing the food, but I said I would pick up a bottle of Cava and some soft drinks.

Chapter 5

A few hours later I was back in the same carpark where I met with Marc originally. The picnic site that he had suggested is around a 30 minute walk from here. It was a beautiful day, and I was happy to be out walking. I still felt a little cold following my earlier river swim, so a good walk would be beneficial to me.

Marc walked up armed with a picnic basket and a rucksack. He placed them on the floor, took hold of my hand, and pulled me to him for a kiss on the lips. It was nice and he had a lovely smile which lit up his features.

"How are you Lily?" he asked.

"I'm great thanks. I've actually had a really busy day so far. How are you?" I reciprocated.

"I'm good too thanks. Tell me about your day," Marc replied.

I filled Marc in on my busy morning. He seemed quite impressed by my new PB and my river swim adventure. He told me that he'd had a chilled morning as Sunday is usually his long run day. He's currently training for an ultra marathon later this year, so he would be running twenty miles tomorrow. That seems like a really long way to me.

By now we'd been walking for a few minutes and I felt warm again. We'd traversed the park and scrambled down to the river bank and were now walking along the tow path. Like last week, there were some rowers out on the water again. This time however, we turned off the river bank and over a stile and followed a footpath through some fields. I hadn't been here before, and it was truly stunning. Beautiful meadows with gorgeous, proud trees. Dotted here and there were a number of picnic benches. Surprisingly there was hardly anyone around. I could only see a couple of other people strolling in the distance. I was mesmerised by the amazing patchwork of green colours made by the trees and grass.

We made our way over to a picnic bench and Marc deposited the food and drinks on the table. He took out a picnic blanket and spread it out next to the table, and then proceeded to take hold of the Cava that I had purchased. A pop of the cork and he filled up two plastic flutes and handed one to me. I took an initial sip of the bubbles and smiled. I had chosen well as it was a really nice, flavoursome, dry Cava.

"Cheers," said Marc as he tapped glasses with me. "Here's to a lovely afternoon in the sunshine."

"Cheers," I responded.

I felt quite content. Marc seemed to be a nice guy, he was fairly good looking and sporty which is of course important to me. He had good manners and I was looking forward to getting to know him a little more. Dare I say it, he wasn't quite as good looking as Jack, but then where did that get me? It was time to make some changes and I didn't want to repeat past mistakes.

We sat down on the picnic blanket and Marc opened the hamper. He'd provided a pretty impressive picnic. There was a lovely looking baguette, there was roast chicken (he'd bought a cooked one from the supermarket and then taken all the meat off the bone). There were strawberries, cucumber and a few types of cheeses and crackers. It was a positive feast. I was expecting a couple of sandwiches and a packet of crisps, so this was a lovely surprise.

We chatted lightly and a few minutes later, when I'd finished my first glass of fizz, came the dreaded question.

"How long have you been single?" asked Marc.

I sighed. "I split up from my last boyfriend around three months ago. How about you?" I hoped that redirecting the query back to him would stave off any further discomforting questions.

"I've been single for about a year now," replied Marc. "I was in that relationship for nearly ten years though, so it was a big change. I needed to be on my own for a while afterwards, so this is only the second date that I've been on in a very long time."

"What are you looking for from a relationship now then," I asked.

"Nothing too heavy, but I would like to find a partner to share the good times with. I don't think I'd like to get too serious just yet, but I do miss the companionship and having fun with someone special."

At that, Marc offered up the Cava, so I held up my flute for a refill. As I sipped slowly on my glass, I pondered what my answer to the same question would be. It's tricky because I am thirty now, I would like a family at some point and I am aware that my biological clock is ticking. Conversely, I don't want to jump into anything too quickly before I've had a chance to really get to know someone. It's ok for men, they don't have quite the same time pressures that us ladies have.

"You have beautiful eyes," said Marc staring thoughtfully at me. He's very hot on eye contact, which I do like. Eye contact is a great way to convey to someone that you are attracted to them. I think I'd like Marc to kiss me and as that thought embeds in my head, I see his eyes flutter down to my lips. That's a sure fire sign that he is thinking about kissing me too.

I leant forwards a little and Marc leant in to me and we shared our first kiss. He tasted lightly of Cava and was nice and gentle. His lips were soft and his tongue lightly explored my mouth in a sensual way. A good kiss is really important and I get very much put off if someone is too aggressive or full on when they kiss.

We broke apart and both sipped our fizz. We smiled at each other, both seemingly happy in the moment. Suddenly, carnage broke out. Just as I heard someone whistling and calling, I got pushed sharply from behind. A beautiful black labrador puppy bounded around me, stuck his snout into the food basket and knocked over the remaining Cava. He was soon joined by another seemingly identical labrador that pushed over my plastic flute and slobbered down my top. Distracted, I leapt up and managed to catch the corner of the picnic blanket at the same time. As I stood up the blanket was pulled hard, and everything that wasn't already displaced then toppled over. What a mess.

Running footsteps accompanied a worried looking man holding a dog leash with a splitter line.

"I'm so sorry to have interrupted you. The pups ran off and wouldn't come back. I'm so sorry." He explained. The man surveyed the carnage and smacked his forehead with his hand. "What was I doing? Why did I let them off the lead?"

He seemed incredibly sorry about what had happened. The dogs eagerly jumped up at him, not realising that they were in trouble. They thought it was a great game, and one had cheese on his whiskers and the other had polished off some of the chicken.

"Don't worry, they are gorgeous," I reassured. "What are their names?"

"The boy is called Jasper and the girl is called Lexi. They are only a year old and are right little tearaways. And my name is George," replied the man. "And once again, please accept my apologies. I'm so sorry to have ruined your picnic."

"They are beautiful bundles of fun," I stated. "And don't worry. It's not too much bother. They just thought it was a good game."

By this point both the pups were back on the lead, and George pulled them away.

"Come on pups, time to go home," he said. "Let's leave these nice people in peace."

As George walked away, I heard a big sigh from Marc.

"I hate dogs," said Marc. "They are such a pain in the ass."

Oh no. This was a massive red flag. I love dogs, and I just don't understand anyone that doesn't feel the same.

"The food is ruined now," he complained. "And they've knocked over the last of the Cava. They've ruined our picnic."

"It's not an issue," I placated. "A good picnic is really about the company, not the food. And we both have to drive, so it's probably best that we didn't finish the Cava anyway."

"But the food is a disaster. And we hadn't even started eating," grumbled Marc. "Bloody dogs. It should be illegal to have them off a lead."

I couldn't believe that he truly thought that. Dogs should be allowed to run free and have fun. And we were in the middle of the countryside. It was just unfortunate that they had ended up in the midst of our picnic. I thought it was quite entertaining, but Marc clearly had sense of humour failure.

Well, that put a real dampener on proceedings. As we packed things up, Marc continued to grumble, so I suggested that we head back towards the cars. I'd totally switched off to Marc now, and wondered quite what I'd seen in him in the first place. He had behaved like a sulky child and now I just wanted to go home. But first, I had a thirty minute walk with Mr Grumpy to contend with.

A short time later, I gave a sigh of relief as I sat in my car and texted Molly.

Please tell me you are free tonight and we can go out. I've just had a nightmare date with Marc.

Within about fifteen seconds my phone rang, and I answered it while watching Marc leave the car park.

"What happened, Lily?" asked Molly. "Are you ok?"

"I'm fine Molly. Just had a bit of a disastrous date that's all," I replied.

I proceeded to fill Molly in on what had happened. I explained that the issue was not what had happened, but the way that Marc dealt with it. Molly too thought the dogs joining the party was quite funny, but could totally see why I'd got 'the ick' with Marc. And once you get the ick you know the relationship is doomed.

"Can we go out tonight?" I asked. "I feel like letting my hair down and getting blasted."

"I was supposed to be going out with Harry, but I'm sure he will understand that I need some girlie time," Molly replied.

Honestly, Molly is just the best. I don't know how I'd cope without her support. She is always there when I need her.

I started the car up and headed home. I felt cheered up and excited again, with a night out in front of me.

Chapter 6

"Here you are, Lily. Get this down you," laughed Molly.

She handed me two baby Guinness cocktails. These are shots made of Tia Maria and Baileys and they look like a tiny pint of Guinness. They look and taste delightful. We were seated at a table in the busy cocktail bar in town and Molly had just been to the bar to get us a Prosecco each. I didn't know that she was getting the baby Guinness shots as well, but I was immensely grateful.

We clinked the glasses together and took the first of the shots. She then gestured for me to take the second. As I did so, I caught the eye of a tall, dark, rather handsome looking man standing alone at the bar looking directly at me.

I wiped my mouth to make sure that I didn't have any remnants of the drinks and picked up the Prosecco for my first sip.

"Don't look now, but there's a cute guy over there," I said to Molly.

"I hate it when you say that," replied Molly. "I'm gagging to turn around and stare at him now."

"Well, you'll just have to contain yourself," I laughed. I was glad that I'd sat this side, so that I could look freely at the cute guy without being too obvious.

"So, do you think you will hear from Marc again?" questioned Molly.

"I doubt it," I replied. "I think he realised that I wasn't overly impressed by his behaviour. I'd be quite surprised if I did hear from him again."

"He did go to quite some effort with the picnic though," commented Molly.

"Yes, that is true. But I just got the ick at his attitude. He really did come across as a spoilt child who didn't get his own way," I said.

"I get what you mean," agreed Molly. "Life throws issues at us all the time. It's how you deal with them that is important. Getting in a mood because things don't go to plan is hardly ideal."

I could see that the cute guy was still looking regularly across at us, and I was momentarily distracted which Molly quickly picked up on.

"I'm just heading to the ladies, so I can check out your guy," said Molly. "What's he wearing?"

I explained where the cute guy was and what he was wearing, so that Molly would easily pick him out. Molly then jumped up and started weaving through the tables towards the restrooms.

I picked up my drink and sipped thoughtfully. I wasn't really bothered that things hadn't gone well with Marc. I was pleased that I had got out for my first date since things had gone wrong with Jack. It showed me that I am at least open to meeting someone new. I'd had enough of being sad now – it was definitely time to move forwards.

Molly soon came back from the ladies, and I realised that the cute guy had disappeared from my view. I hoped that he hadn't left the bar and would be back shortly. The bar had been filling up and it was quite busy, so if he'd needed another drink he would have to move to get one. I hoped that was the case rather than he'd gone home or moved on elsewhere.

"Your man is indeed cute, and no wedding ring either," said Molly.

"I can't see him now though," I stated.

"Don't worry, he has just moved around the bar to be served. I bet he will be back shortly," said Molly.

A few minutes later Molly was proved correct. The cute guy was indeed back, and as I looked across at him he smiled directly at me. Well, I hoped it was at me anyway. I resisted the urge to look behind me to see if there was anyone else there.

I could see that he had moved on from the lager he had previously been drinking. He now had a bottle of Prosecco on the bar next to him. In fact, on second glance, it wasn't Prosecco but was actually a bottle of Champagne. He must be posh.

The cute man started to walk towards me carrying his Champagne and a single flute.

"Hello ladies, how are you both?" he asked. "I was wondering if you would like to join me for a glass of champagne? I hate to drink alone."

"Um," I started to say, but was interrupted by Molly.

"We'd love to," said Molly. "Please do sit down. I'm Molly and this is my friend Lily. What's your name?"

"My name is Leo," said the cute guy. "It's a pleasure to meet you both. Do sup up your glasses and I'll refill you with champagne."

We both picked up our glasses and finished the last remaining sips and held them aloft for him to pour.

"I'm sorry to gatecrash your evening," said Leo. "I was due to meet my sister, but she's bailed on me. She's just had her first novel published, so I bought the champagne to celebrate. But it seems she got a better offer."

I laughed. "That's a bit harsh," I say. "Dumping your brother when he's gone to the effort of buying champagne."

"I think so too," laughed Leo. "But things often happen for a reason." He then gave me a wink, which made my heart race just a little bit.

We started to chit chat and find out a little about each other. Leo explained that he is an architect (what is it about architects??). He's only recently moved to the area, and it's his first visit to this cocktail bar. He told us that he is single, and lives alone in a village just the other side of Castledyke. And he has a border collie called Bob.

He seemed like an interesting man and I enjoyed chatting with him. Molly was happy to take a backseat and let the two of us converse. In fact, I could see that she was busy texting.

"Lily, do you mind if Harry joins us?" she asked.

"Of course not," I replied. "It would be nice to see him."

I could see that Molly was feeling a bit like a lemon now that Leo had joined us. It made sense for Harry to join us as well.

"Who is Harry?" asked Leo.

"Harry is my boyfriend," replied Molly.

"How about you Lily. Do you have a partner?" asked Leo.

"No," I replied. "I'm very single at the moment."

"Well that's good to know," replied Leo. He looked me straight in the eye and smiled. He was definitely flirting with me.

"So what do you like doing in your free time?" asked Leo.

"I enjoy running and swimming. I've recently started wild swimming which is much more fun than swimming in a pool. I love to ski. To be honest I like most sports really and I'm up for trying most things. How about you?" I asked.

"I'm not much of a runner, but I enjoy rowing and I go to the gym regularly. I actually really enjoy photography, so spend a lot of my free time out and about with my camera," explained Leo.

I found that very interesting indeed and start asking him more about his photography. He told me that he loves to travel abroad and around the UK taking pictures of buildings. And of course, being an architect, he's perfectly placed to enjoy his hobby alongside his profession. He's actually a really engaging man, and I enjoyed talking to him.

A few minutes later Harry joined us, and Molly carried out introductions. I headed off to the bar to buy the next bottle of Prosecco and get a lager for Harry. He's not a big fan of drinking wine and prefers to stick to a pint. Leo joined us on the Prosecco and we continued chatting.

A little later it's Harry's turn to the bar. He bought us another bottle of Prosecco and a baby Guiness each. I'm starting to feel rather tipsy by this point and find myself doing rather a lot of staring into Leo's eyes. He moved his chair around closer to me and kept touching his leg onto mine. I liked it, and found myself flirting more and more with him. The alcohol most probably contributed to the situation.

I needed to pop to the ladies, so I stood up and gestured to Molly where I'm going. She immediately arose and we started to wind our way through the tables across the room. I felt rather wobbly and bumped my leg into the corner of a table as I went. I felt rather worse for wear now that I was stood up, and I began to regret drinking quite as much as I had. As we headed into the ladies, I caught the door frame with my shoulder and ricocheted into the door itself. Ouch.

That hurt. I decided that I had better rein in the drinking a little bit.

A few minutes later Molly and I headed back towards the table. I redirected to the bar and asked for a pint of water. The bartender kindly handed it over, and I sat down next to Leo with my water.

"Are you ok?" he asked concerned.

"Yes, I'm fine," I replied. "Just had a little too much to drink I think."

I surveyed the table. There were multiple empty bottles, a load of shot glasses as well as a number of champagne flutes. I suddenly realised that I had consumed far too much alcohol, and decided that I needed to go home.

"Are you ok, Lily?" asked Molly.

"Yes, I think I need to leave. Are you coming home?" I replied.

"If it's ok with you I'll go back to Harry's," she said. "Perhaps Leo could walk you home?"

"I'd be glad to," stated Leo. "I'd like to make sure that you get home safely and I promise to be a gentleman."

"OK, thanks," I replied. "That's kind of you."

I said goodbye to Molly and Harry, and Leo took my hand and led me out of the bar. It felt good to hold hands with him. I'm quite a tactile kind of person, and I enjoy being looked after.

It's about a twenty minute walk back home and I started to feel much better. The pint of water had done its job and Leo is good company. He chattered away about a forthcoming trip he's taking to California. He told me that he had done quite a lot of work across the pond, and he enjoyed regular trips out there.

A short time later we were in the kitchen and we decided we were both hungry. We agreed on bacon sandwiches, so I popped some bacon in the air fryer and some bread in the toaster. A short time later we both munched on our sandwiches, drank a cup of tea and continued to chat. Once the sandwiches were devoured, we started to kiss. Leo is a great kisser, and even better, he tasted of bacon and Baileys. It's a nice taste, and I was keen to keep kissing. In fact, I decided that I'd quite like to take Leo to bed.

I pulled on his hand and led him into my bedroom.

Chapter 7

I pulled Leo towards me, and we started kissing. At the same time, I walked him backwards until he'd reached my bed, and I pushed against his chest until he's sitting. I moved my knees either side of him until I'm straddled on his lap and we still continued to kiss. Kissing is so important. It's a proper skill that not enough people have.

Leo then took charge, and he pulled me across him until I'm lying on the bed and then he manoeuvred me upright so that he could pull off my top. I'm glad that I had the foresight to wear decent underwear and not the comfy pants that I usually wore. I've got on a set of red lingerie that is pretty sexy and I'm feeling confident.

In turn, I also pulled Leo's shirt over his head. He's got a nice figure. He's slim and he's toned but he's not ripped. He looked like he works out, but not excessively.

"You are so beautiful Lily," he murmured. "And you have beautiful breasts."

"Well thank you, Leo. You are pretty hot yourself," I replied.

Leo rather expertly unhooked my bra around my back with a single motion. He's obviously very lucky or fairly experienced.

"That was professionally done," I commented to him.

"Perhaps a little lucky," he replied with a laugh.

Leo then started to kiss me again, and nuzzled a trail down my neck, past my shoulder blades and down to my breast. Then he took my nipple into his mouth and gently sucked and explored with his tongue. At the same time his hand followed down from my waist and started rubbing me through my jeans. I was already turned on as it's been a few months since I had any action in the physical department. Whilst my head might not have been ready for anything until now, my body had been missing the great sex that I had previously enjoyed with Jack.

Damn, I hadn't thought about Jack for the last couple of hours. And now he's popped into my head. I turned my thoughts back to Leo, and just tried to savour the moment.

Leo quietly asked if he could remove my jeans, and I lifted my hips in response. He undid the zip and slipped the jeans down over my hips and pulled them down my legs. As he got to my feet, he made sure to also tug off my socks so all I was still wearing was my necklace and my red thong.

"Wow," said Leo. "You truly are something else."

I felt really happy at receiving the compliments from Leo. And the benefit of lying on your back is that it makes you look nice and slim. I could even see my stomach muscles, so felt quite proud. The efforts that I have made over the past year or so with regards to my running has really paid off. I've lost the excess pounds that I was carrying, I've toned up and gained a lot more definition. And Leo certainly seemed to appreciate it.

Leo continued kissing down my body until I could feel his warm breath through my pants. He used a single finger to tug the front of the thong sideways, and he used his tongue to lick around my clit. Jesus, it felt sensational. It had been a while since I'd had any sexual attention, and my body was certainly responding.

Leo was gently slipping his tongue inside and around me and he then pressed his finger inside me. What a sensation. I was starting to feel hotter and hotter and I could tell how wet I had become.

"You taste beautiful," murmured Leo. "I could do this all day."

"Well I certainly couldn't," I replied. "I'm so close to having an orgasm already."

It was time to take some more clothes off Leo. I undid the buckle of his trousers and slid them down his legs. He kicked them off his ankles, and I made sure to take off his socks. His shaft sprung to attention creating a significant bulge in his boxers. He clearly had no issues in the erection department.

"Do you have any condoms with you by any chance?" I asked.

"Bugger, I don't," replied Leo. "I'm so sorry."

"That's ok, I have a box hidden away in a cupboard. Just give me two ticks and I will go and grab them."

I jumped up and went to a chest of drawers in the corner of the room. In one of the drawers was my emergency stash of condoms. They had probably been there a while, but I'm sure they would do the job. I carried the box over to the bed and took one out. I ripped the wrapper and laid the condom on top ready for its use shortly. Leo had wriggled out of his boxers by this point, reached for the condom and slid it on. He was rock solid and looking very ready for action.

I had straddled Leo on the bed and he took hold of me and rotated us both around until I was on my back and he hovered over the top of me. However, rather than enter me, he took hold of my leg and gently hooked it over his shoulder. This made me feel incredibly horny and I felt the tip of him as he pushed into my opening. Whilst I was by this time very wet, I felt really tight, and Leo manoeuvred himself around a little and then took hold of his shaft with his hand to ensure a smooth entry inside me.

He ever so slowly pushed inside me, and I could feel my opening expand to accommodate him. He certainly was a well endowed man, and I was feeling every centimetre of him as he started to fill me up. The position we were in made me feel quite vulnerable, so I needed to say something.

"Just take it very slowly please," I requested.

"I fully intend to," replied Leo. "I'd like to savour this experience if that's ok."

And with that I could feel him increasing the pressure and gently but firmly sliding inside to my very core. It wasn't that he was massively long in length, but he had a very substantial girth. Now that he was inside me, I was less worried, and really starting to revel in the sensation he gave me. It was pretty intense and very fulfilling.

He started to rhythmically but slowly pull out and then push in to me again. He was very controlled and steady, but I could feel the pressure inside me start to build up. It had been a long time since I'd had any action and my body was therefore responding rather quicker than normal. The position we were in provided very deep penetration with great clit stimulation, so I was going to orgasm in no time at all if something didn't change.

Thankfully, Leo was also starting to get rather excited, so I felt him withdraw from me and ask me to turn around. I knelt on all fours and it took no time at all for him to slide his full length into me from behind. He managed to get even deeper penetration from this angle, and it felt absolutely mind-blowing. He cusped my breast with his right hand and I could feel him kissing the back of my neck. The warmth of his breath floated over me and created a sensation in itself.

I slowly sank down but kept my bottom raised, quickly shoving a pillow underneath my middle. I was therefore almost lying down but maintaining a great access point for Leo. Within a couple of minutes Leo had sped up the action and was thrusting deeply inside me. I could feel the orgasm building and this time there was no turning back. Just as I could feel that I was about to tip over the edge, Leo pushed his hand underneath me and applied pressure onto my clit. That was it, it was game over for me. I buried my head into the bed as the orgasm engulfed me. Just a few seconds later I could feel Leo starting to cum. His moans increased as mine were beginning to subside. Neither of us quite contained the pleasure that we were in.

Leo collapsed on top of me, and I felt rather squashed, hot and sweaty. He was still inside of me, so he carefully withdrew and dealt with the condom. He then lay next to me, slung an arm over the top of me, and started to allow his breathing to recover. We both spent the next few moments enjoying that awesome, relaxed feeling that you get after a good orgasm. It was definitely time for rest now, and I soon dropped off into a deep sleep.

Chapter 8

I woke up abruptly. I lay quietly and tried to figure out what woke me. I couldn't hear anything, so I lifted my head from the pillow. I felt a little bit rough with a cloudy head and I felt slightly nauseous. I suddenly remembered about bringing Leo home, so I slowly rolled over expecting him to be lying next to me. There was just an empty space, with a dent in the pillow. Had he left? Or was he in the bathroom perhaps? Or elsewhere in the flat? I laid still and listened to see if I could hear any movement. Nothing.

I climbed steadily out of bed and headed for my dressing gown. Once that was on, I padded around the flat, checking to see if he was in the bathroom, the kitchen or the living room. He was nowhere to be seen, so I guessed that I was woken up by the noise of him leaving. I couldn't see evidence of a note either which seemed a little rude.

In the kitchen, I reached for a glass, poured myself a pint of water and grabbed some ibuprofen from the cupboard. I'd wanted a Diet Coke, but I'd run out, so I made do with water. Having downed the tablets with water, I padded back into my bedroom and crawled back into bed. I reach for my phone which was plugged into the charger next to my bed.

There is a text from Molly.

How's the head, Lily? You seemed a little worse for wear last night. Did you have a good night with Leo?

I sank back into the pillow and started typing a response.

All good thanks. I feel ok, just a little fuzzy. We had a good night, but he must have slipped out first thing because he's not here now.

A couple of minutes later, Molly called.

"I couldn't be bothered to type, it seemed easier to call," said Molly.

"No worries, it's nicer to chat anyway," I replied.

"So tell me all. Walk me through the rest of the evening," said Molly.

I told Molly that I had successfully sobered up on the walk home, assisted by the bacon sandwich. I then proceeded to give her a bit of a rundown of the night's activities, well, a shortened version anyway.

"And he just left this morning?" Molly asked.

"Well, yes, I think so. I woke up about fifteen minutes ago by a noise which I'm guessing was the door closing as he left."

"And he's not left a note or anything?"

"Nothing," I replied. "Or not that I've noticed anyway."

"That's a bit odd don't you think? Did you get his phone number last night?" Molly asked.

"No, I didn't," I replied thoughtfully. "In fact, I don't even know his last name. All I know about him is that he is an architect. I don't know his surname, where he lives or where he works. I don't think I have anyway of getting hold of him again."

"Oh, no," exclaimed Molly. "That's not good. You two seemed to get on like a house on fire. I never would have left you to go home alone with him if I hadn't thought he was a genuinely decent guy. Are you sure he didn't perhaps take your number Lily?"

"Um, not that I can remember," I replied. "But I can't be 100% certain. I can't remember telling him my surname either, but I did tell him where I worked and of course he will know where we live."

"Well, we will have to hope that he makes contact with you in due course then. It's a bit annoying that you just have to hope that he does," said Molly.

We continued chatting, and a few minutes later we wrapped up the conversation. Deep down I was a little upset that I didn't have any way of getting hold of Leo. I really did like him. In fact, I never would have had sex with him if I'd know he might disappear without trace. That's certainly not my normal behaviour. I'd only once before slept with a guy on the first night, and we had ended up dating for quite some time.

I'd have to keep my fingers crossed that he gets hold of me somehow. I really had thought there was something special between us. I understand that love at first sight is probably a myth, but when you experience a profound connection with someone it does give you hope. We've all met those rare individuals who insist they knew they were meant to be together from the moment they met. I just hope that it would happen to me.

I'll have to make sure that Molly and I go back to the same venue next weekend, and hope that Leo is in there again. That is if I don't hear from him before then.

Anyway, back to the present. It's time to get my arse out of bed. Today I planned on going for a run (admittedly it will be a steady one!) and perhaps have a little dip in the river this afternoon. That's a sure fire way to get rid of any remaining traces of a hangover. Then, I'd planned a spot of housework and a chill out with Molly tonight.

That evening, I finished cooking a meal for Molly and me. I'd cooked fusilli pasta with chicken breast, broccoli, green beans, sweetcorn and peas in a light cheese sauce. It was scrumptious as well as quick and easy to prepare. I'm definitely not a chef in any way, shape or form. My limited repertoire of meals consists of about seven basic dishes, a full English and a Sunday roast. However, at least it's fairly healthy and I don't have a sweet tooth so rarely eat desserts.

Molly had contributed a really nice bottle of Pinot Grigio (in fact there was another one chilling in the fridge), so we idly chatted and put the world to rights. We'd already talked through the early departure from Leo and we were both hopeful that I'd see him again in the future. Molly still said that she felt bad that she'd left me alone with him. I'd had to reassure her that at thirty years old, I'm a big girl, and quite capable of looking after myself.

"You are just having a bit of a rubbish time of it at the moment," said Molly. "First there was Marc, who didn't exactly light your fire, but seemed alright until the picnic. And then you seemed to hit it off with the magical Leo, who then disappeared without trace."

"Well, we don't know that he has disappeared," I stated. "He might come back, or message me or make contact somehow. And Marc was no big loss. It was only a couple of dates, and anyone that doesn't like dogs is a big red flag in my opinion. I truly don't understand people that don't like dogs. They are just the most amazing loving and giving animals. What's not to love?"

I'm quite aware that I had probably kidded myself about Leo. It seems that modern dating is very different nowadays. It's a few years since I dated as I was with Jack for a year and then Rob for a couple of years before that. I'd not really been on the dating scene since my early twenties, and it seems much more casual now than it was back then.

Of course, I watch dating and reality shows on the TV, but they aren't like real life. Look at Love Island. A bunch of amazingly attractive people who are way more interested in being famous than finding love. And it works. At least half of them go on to be influencers, or fashion designers and never work a real job again. However, not many of them seem to find the love that they are supposedly looking for. They seem to keep popping up on different reality TV dating shows time and time again.

Throughout the rest of the evening, we moved onto other conversations. We managed to polish off the two bottles of wine between us. And then it was time for bed. Back to work tomorrow so we both needed some beauty sleep.

Chapter 9

Friday night came around quickly and probably not surprisingly, I'd not heard anything from Leo. I was putting a brave face on the situation, but deep down I was a little gutted. We really had connected so well, and I was quite upset that he'd not made contact.

I'd had a look on social media and LinkedIn but it's almost impossible to find someone without a surname. I'd looked at the Facebook page of the cocktail bar, but there were no Leos listed there. I'd looked up Architects on LinkedIn around Castledyke but not seen any sign of a Leo listed there either. But without more specific information, it's like looking for a needle in a haystack.

Just in case he might be there, Molly and I popped into the cocktail bar on Friday night, but to no avail. Whilst the bar was busy, I wasn't really in the frame of mind to be sociable, so we didn't stay too long. There was no sign of Leo, so we just had a glass of wine each and then decided to go home instead. Molly hadn't really wanted to come out at all, and only did so as she is such a good friend to me. So Molly headed off to Harry's and I headed home with a bottle of wine from the off-licence.

I was tempted to re-enact the Bridget Jones scene where she's in her pyjamas singing 'All by Myself' by Jamie O'Neal. But I wasn't really that sad. It was just a temporary blip. Instead, I decided to watch the movie 'Ted' which is hilarious and then I gave myself a bit of a stern talking to. It was time to forget about Leo. I needed to chalk the whole thing up to experience and to learn from my mistakes. Time to move on.

No more sleeping with someone that I've just met. No more sleeping with a guy that I don't know anything about. Initially, I'd thought the whole thing was a romantic, exciting experience. And now that I knew he'd disappeared without trace, it felt rather seedy and I felt slightly exploited. Admittedly, it was my own fault. I'm not trying to blame Leo. I was the one that drank too much. I was the one that invited him back home with me, and assured Molly I was fine on my own. And I was the one that led him to bed. He had behaved like a gentleman the whole evening. And he was very giving and thoughtful in bed. It was only the disappearance in the morning that was upsetting. I'd gone from thinking it would be an exciting story to tell the grandkids to feeling a little ashamed about my actions. Well, time to grow up and move on.

Sometimes I let my imagination run away with me. I pin hopes and dreams onto someone that I've just met. It's not really falling hard for them. It's about falling for a perception that you have of them. It's not really them, in fact I don't know them at all. I have no idea if they are loyal, honest, hard-working or have any of the characteristics that I've given them in my imagination. So, when they let me down, there is no need to feel disappointed. Leo didn't let me down. I let myself down. I tell myself that it won't happen again. That I've learnt from my past mistakes. That I must truly get to know someone before allowing my feelings to develop. But then I also think that you have to open yourself up to love, or it won't ever happen. If you have too much of a wall up, no-one will be bothered to get to know the real you. I guess age and experience helps you find the middle ground. Or maybe it's just pot luck. Maybe some people meet someone that is just right for them. And some people don't. Who knows?

I woke up Saturday morning to the sound of raindrops on the window. We'd been lucky with the weather recently, and most weekends had been dry. I guess it's inevitable that it must rain sometimes. Still, it's not that heavy so I decided that I would head to parkrun as normal.

A couple of hours later I wandered into the park. Going to parkrun always cheered me up as I now knew so many of the people that both volunteered and ran parkrun. In fact, as I arrived, I saw one of my friends, Lucy, who is the Run Director for today. She's recently joined the core team that organises Castledyke parkrun and she was in a bit of a fluster. She told me that she was short of volunteers and only had one barcode scanner. I immediately offered to volunteer instead of running today. I'd already run a few times this week, so it was no hardship to take a step back from the running and help out instead. I'd started volunteering occasionally a couple of months back and it had been incredibly rewarding. I'd started out with marshalling points of the course, but now I enjoyed helping at the start/finish area such as handing out the finish tokens, barcode scanning or timekeeping. The best part was that I had integrated into the parkrun community so much better by volunteering, and as a result every Saturday morning felt like meeting up with family.

As the runners set off around the 5km course, I spent the first ten minutes clapping and encouraging as they went past. I waved to James who was doing a great run, looking like he was going to be about twentieth over the line. It was nice to see James, and maybe I'd get to go for a coffee with him after parkrun this week as I had no pressing engagements. As the lead runner went past for the second time, it was time to get into position for barcode scanning. I was equipped with the parkrun volunteer app on my mobile phone, and I had a physical box for collecting up the finish tokens once the individual runners had been scanned.

In no time at all, I was busy scanning the lead runners. They were out of breath but smiling, happy with their achievements. There was a lot of camaraderie between the runners as many of them know each other well. If they didn't before they started running parkrun, they soon get to know each other. A number of them enquired if I was well, and it was nice to have a brief chat. Once James had completed, he came over and presented me with his personal barcode followed by his finish token. Once scanned he dropped them in the box, then asked if I had time to meet for a coffee when I'd finished.

"That sounds great, James," I replied. "I'd love to meet with you once I've finished scanning."

"Great," responded James. "I'm going to nip home for a shower and will meet you in the café in say half an hour?"

"That's perfect," I confirmed. "I will look forward to seeing you shortly."

Today there were about 180 runners, so it took some time for everyone to complete. Once finished, I duly uploaded the results and then helped pack up the finish funnel. I then bid farewell to the remaining volunteers and runners and headed for the park exit. I walked the couple of streets to the café that James and I have previously met at for breakfast.

I had dated James for a few weeks but he'd still been hung up on his ex-girlfriend at the time. When she moved back from the United States, he'd chosen to revisit that relationship, and I had soon moved on with Jack. Sadly for James, the relationship with his ex hadn't flourished and within a few weeks it had fizzled out. By that time of course, I had more than moved on with Jack, so there was no option of rekindling things.

And now that things had ended between Jack and I, James had a new girlfriend that he was happy with. It seemed that timing was always off between us – but we had remained good friends and I very much valued that friendship.

Twenty minutes later I pushed open the café door, listening to the chime of the bells. The café was busy and I tentatively scanned the room looking for James. I spotted him over by the far wall and headed across to him. I recognised a number of the patrons from parkrun. There were plenty of parkrun branded t-shirts and scuffed trainers in evidence. As I weaved my way through the tables, I said hi to a couple of familiar faces.

As I approached James, I could see his face brighten up and the twinkle in his eye as he smiled at me. He is genuinely a nice guy, really warm and friendly. Just as I reached him, a man at the next table stood up, abruptly pushing back his chair. It caught my leg and sent me reeling head-first pretty much into James's lap. I unfortunately caught my nose on the corner of the table and a great burst of blood suddenly spurted out. Accompanying the quite incredible fountain of blood was excruciating pain which made me stumble backwards until I ended up sitting on my arse backed up against the next door's table leg.

At this point, my nose was so painful that I didn't care that I looked like a complete numpty. Well, a complete red numpty anyway. Who knew that so much blood could escape so quickly from one's nose?

James jumped up, held out his hands and hauled me upright before turning me around and sitting me down in his chair. I was in a bit of a daze, so James handed me some napkins to try and stem the flow. The floor looked like a mini-massacre had taken place and much of the table too. The nearby patrons started collecting up their napkins and handing them to James, while the waitress hurried over with a towel.

A few minutes later, normality had restored. I was still holding tissues to my nose to stop the blood flow, but the waitress had mopped up the blood from the floor and wiped the table clean with antibacterial spray. What a palaver.

The pain had ebbed away by this time, and I just felt a little dazed and like a bit of a fool. James assured me that it could have happened to anyone, and the man that had caused the incident by jumping up so quickly was so apologetic. The other patrons had returned to their chats and the general buzz of noise had returned to the café. It could have happened to anyone but why did it have to happen to me?

James asked me what I wanted to order, so I snuffled quietly that I would like a cup of tea and a bacon sandwich please. The waitress took our order and assured me that it wouldn't be long. James then took the seat opposite me, and we finally managed to start a chat.

"So, Lily. Aside from the last ten minutes, how have you been?" asked James.

"Much better thanks James," I replied. "Things are looking up, and I've moved on from Jack now. I've settled into my new home with Molly, I've made new friends, I've got my running back on track and even work is going pretty well at the moment. How about you?"

"Well, my running is better now that I've finally managed to shift the hamstring injury that I had for a few months. And work is ok. But things seem to be fizzling out with Nat. We seem to be drifting apart somewhat, although there is nothing specific that I could put my finger on," said James.

"I'm sorry to hear that," I replied. And actually, I was. James is a great guy, and I'd like to see him happy. On the plus side, maybe there might be a chance for us to rekindle things? I certainly wouldn't entertain going down that route until he was definitely single again.

"It is what it is," said James. "We've had a fun few months, but maybe it's just a bit of fun rather than anything more deep and meaningful. Maybe the relationship has run its course. Time will tell I guess. Anyway, how about you. Have you started dating again?"

I laughed. I gave James a very brief synopsis on my dates with Marc and said that I wouldn't be seeing him again. I didn't tell him about Leo though. I felt awkward about that. I wasn't feeling very proud of myself and felt that was a story to keep to myself.

"Well, it's good that you are getting back out there," said James. "Onwards and upwards now."

"Exactly," I agreed. "To be honest, I'm quite happy just doing my own thing at the moment. It's nice to have my independence again, and just do what I want when I want without having to consider anyone else's feelings or schedule."

"I know what you mean. It's really not all that bad being single is it?" agreed James.

"It's not at all. If it wasn't for the fact that I would like to have a family one day, I think I'd happily stay single."

"You could always go for the single mum route? Or perhaps adopt?" suggested James. "There are plenty of children looking for a loving home."

"I have looked into it briefly," I replied. "And although I do think it's an amazing thing to do, I still have hopes that I can stick to the traditional family unit of mum, dad and kids. I'm only thirty years old, so I'm not exactly over the hill. Although I do appreciate that my biological clock is ticking away. It's alright for you men – you can keep having children until you are ancient – assuming you're able to keep attracting younger women of course."

James laughed. "I guess we do have that benefit."

We had a pause in conversation to start eating our food. James had also opted for a bacon sandwich although he had egg with his as well. The food in this café is really good. Really nice bread cooked on the premises. Proper thick bacon, and oodles of ketchup. You can't beat a proper hearty sandwich.

"So how come you weren't running this morning?" enquired James.

"Well, I was intending to," I replied gesturing to my leggings and trainers. "But I'm friends with Lucy, today's Run Director, and she was short of volunteers when I arrived. So I offered to help out rather than run today. It's something I've started doing from time-to-time and I find it very rewarding. It's also enabled me to become friends with so many more of the regulars."

"That's a great idea," mused James. "To be honest, I hadn't really thought much about volunteering before. Maybe it's something I should consider."

"For sure," I nodded. "You really should. It's fun and the people involved are really nice."

"I'll do that," agreed James.

Fifteen minutes later we had finished our breakfast, and it was time to leave. The café was emptying out by this time, and the staff were starting to setup the tables for lunch. As we left the café, James turned to give me a hug.

"Look after yourself, Lily," he said as he hugged me goodbye. "I hope to see you soon."

"Likewise, James," I replied. "It's always good to see you."

At that James headed off back towards the park, and I turned towards the direction of home. A few steps along the pavement I spied a familiar face walking towards me. Was it? Was it? It looked like Leo. Could it be?

It certainly looked like Leo. However, he was busy chatting to a lady that he was holding hands with, and she in turn held hands with a little girl who must have been about four or five. I froze. I stepped to the side of the pavement and watched as they approached me.

It was definitely Leo. I recognised him, I recognised his watch, and I even recognised his walk. As my eyes drifted down to his hand, I could see on his third finger was a wedding ring. Oh my god. I couldn't believe it.

The woman was laughing at something that Leo had said to her. Her eyes were sparkling and she looked happy. The little girl was skipping alongside them, smiling broadly and looking around her. She was a spitting image of Leo, so was clearly his daughter.

I turned my back on them and looked into the window of the shop that I had been walking past. I felt like I'd been sucker punched. I felt physical pain in my stomach. The little family unit of three walked past, without a care in the world, with no idea that I was even there. They were so wrapped up in the moment that they hadn't even noticed me. I turned slowly to look at them from behind, and I could see Leo beaming at the woman, who was still laughing with him. The little girl was still skipping and swinging her arms.

I felt truly devastated. I had slept with a married man. He had blatantly lied to me because he told me that he was single. Why would someone do that? Had he told me any truths at all? Who knew if he was an architect? Had he really been meeting his sister? Was the champagne just a pulling tactic rather than bought to celebrate his sister's first novel? Where was his wife that night? Or more to the point, where did she think he was?

There were fifty questions running through my mind, but I wasn't in any position to get answers to them. They had already gone past me and what would be the point of trying to talk to him? All that would happen is that it would devastate his wife and hurt his little girl. While one part of me wanted him to be caught out, another didn't want to inflict that hurt onto someone else. Onto a wife and an innocent little girl.

I walked home slowly, deep in thought. I was devastated to find out that I'd slept with a married man. I now felt used and abused. What I had thought was a romantic story now felt seedy and dirty. How ridiculous it was that I thought, even just for a fleeting moment, that I might have a future with this man. Talk about projection. Talk about pinning your hopes, dreams and aspirations onto someone else.

It was the reality check that I needed. There was a good lesson to learn here. And that lesson was that it was important to get to know someone before having intimate moments with them. Jumping into bed with the first good-looking guy that paid me attention was not going to get me anywhere – other than heartbreak.

I was better than that. I deserve better than that. I am a good person. I like to help other people. I work hard. I care for my family and friends. I am a great believer in karma. I do believe that 'eventually' what goes around comes around.

A few minutes later, my self-reflection was turning to a more positive approach. Right, this was it. Time to take stock, learn from my mistakes. And move on. By the time I got home, I felt rather better about myself. Yes, I had been naive. Yes, I had behaved like a fool. But, I would pick myself up, dust myself down, and move on.

Chapter 10

I had arranged to meet Rachel and some other Bluetits for a swim, so after gathering my things I strolled towards the river. Thankfully, the drizzle had stopped now, and the sun was trying to break through. The Bluetits were waiting on the jetty for me. There were four of them today. Rachel, Beth, Sara and a new lady called Laura.

As we were getting changed on the jetty, there was lots of chat as always. Honestly, you wouldn't believe what these ladies talk about. There is nothing off limits. But, what happens at the river stays at the river, so unfortunately I can't enlighten you.

A few minutes later we were heading down the ladder into the river. As always, my breath is taken away when I first enter the river. I concentrate on breathing out very slowly and keeping my breathing even and steady. The natural reaction is to hold your breath, but actually this is the worse thing you can do, and only serves to raise your heart rate.

Within ten seconds or so everything had normalised, and I felt good. I tuned back into the chatter and laughed along at some of the stories. We swam upstream for a good few hundred metres. When we got to the summer tree, Rachel, Beth and Laura headed back for the jetty. Sara and I decided to swim on a little further, and practice some front crawl.

I'd recently invested in a tow float, so that was attached around my waist. I'd also got neoprene gloves and socks on for the first time. Sara takes part in triathlons, so she is a really good swimmer and was soon a little further in front than me. As I was feeling tired, I took a little break and trod water. I could see that Sara was around 100m away now, and the other swimmers were halfway back to the jetty.

Suddenly, I felt a bump on my arm, and it was much stronger than a bit of weed or a stick. What was that?

I turned around, and suddenly up popped this large grey head with piercing eyes that stared straight at me, unblinking. Jesus Christ, it was the seal. I was totally shocked and a feeling of delight ran through me. How lucky was I? I'd always wanted to see the seal, and now here he was. Right in front of me.

He swam right around in front of me and bumped into my other arm. He was large but thankfully didn't appear aggressive. I felt him lunge out of the water and then he bumped my hand. He then bumped into my ribcage. The next thing I knew the seal had opened his mouth and placed his jaws either side of my hand. I could feel his tooth pulling on the fabric of my neoprene glove. I'm was very grateful that I was wearing them.

With my other hand, I pushed the seal off me, but he immediately came straight back. It was exactly like a dog jumping up at me, but I had nothing to brace against, so when I tried to push the seal away, he came straight back and I couldn't deter him. He then swam around me in a circle and I felt him graze my ribcage with his jaws. This was starting to worry me now. He's wasn't biting me as such, and oddly it didn't feel aggressive. It reminded me of a puppy that is mouthing you. They are only really exploring you, what you are, figuring out what you are made of. I was very aware, after what Rachel told me, that it would be quite obvious if the seal was being aggressive and he wasn't. I say he, I had no idea if it was a male or female seal. The seal just seemed to be checking me out and then trying to play with me. But, I don't play seal, and I didn't know how to play seal. I'm not sure I really wanted to find out either.

I attempted to swim a few strokes but it's very hard. At least when the seal was right in front of me I knew where he was. But as soon as he moved away, I didn't know where he was or where he was headed and that was almost worse. But he kept coming back for another look and another play. He had another go at my hand, and this time he did bite me. It's wasn't very hard or deep, but it did hurt, and it felt like his tooth had penetrated through my glove and into my hand.

I was getting really concerned now. It had been a couple of minutes and I couldn't seem to get rid of him. I could see that Sara was heading towards me again, but I didn't know if she was even aware of the seal.

"I've got the seal," I called to her.

"What's wrong? What's happening?" Sara called back. "Are you ok?"

"No, I've got the seal and I can't get rid of it," I yelled back.

"Oh my god," called Sara. "Don't panic, I'm on my way. Use your tow float"

Sara bravely started swimming towards me.

I'd forgotten about the tow float. It floated behind me, so I grabbed hold of the cord attaching it to me and pulled it toward me. I pushed it in front of me and used it as a barrier to stop the seal getting close enough to bite me again. The seal had a nibble on the tow float, so I'm thankful that Sara reminded me to use it.

I suddenly had an idea how I might be able to get rid of the seal. I took hold of the tow float and the next time the seal popped up, I bopped him on the head with it. Not too hard, but just enough so that he knows I meant business.

I was right. The seal did not like that. He slipped under the water, and then I didn't know where he was. I continued to tread water and looked around me, wondering where he had gone. I saw some movement in the water about ten metres away, and just for a moment I saw the top of his head before he dived down again. He headed upstream to the left of Sara and seemed to bypass her entirely. I think he'd had enough of playing with humans.

I started swimming towards the jetty. I don't think I'd ever swum this fast before. My heart raced as quickly as it ever had, and I was paranoid that the seal was going to pop up in front of me again. But I made it to the ladder and scrambled out as quickly as possible, closely followed by Sara who had managed to catch me up with her superior swimming skills.

"Oh my god," exclaimed Rachel. "Are you ok? Was that the seal with you?"

I couldn't even speak. My heart was racing, I panted liked I'd just finished the Olympic 100m sprint.

"Yes, yes," I stammered. "That was the seal. And yes, I'm fine. But the seal did bite me."

"Oh my," said Rachel. "Where did it bite you?"

"It bit through my glove. Hold on, once I've caught my breath I'll take a look."

Rachel kindly grabbed my towel for me and dropped it around my shoulders.

I dried off the worst of the water and pulled off my neoprene gloves. Sure enough, there was a small purple puncture mark where the seal's tooth had gone into the top of my hand. It was quite sore although didn't look like very much.

"You will need to make sure that you are up to date on your tetanus vaccination," said Rachel. "Can you remember when you last had one?"

"I've no idea," I responded. "I don't think I've had one since I was a kid. I will have to call the doctors and find out. I guess they will have records with my vaccination details on."

"Yes," agreed Rachel. "That's exactly what you need to do. And quickly. I'm sure there is little to no risk, but it's better to be safe than sorry."

We spent the next few minutes chatting and getting dry and dressed. I'm glad I remembered to bring a flask of tea, as I think that helped me get over the shock of meeting the seal. Despite being bitten, I was glad that I had my seal encounter. Not many people can say they have played with a seal in their natural habitat.

Chapter 11

It was Saturday evening and I'd arranged to meet Molly in the pub for a debrief. I had a fair bit to tell her as she'd been staying at Harry's much of the time recently, so I'd yet to tell her about bumping into Leo and my seal encounter.

As I walked into the pub, Molly, as usual, was already sitting down with a couple of drinks for us, looking as fabulous as she usually does. I'm dressed in jeans, boots and a sparkly top, so actually quite dressed up for me.

After the customary greeting and big hug, I took a seat and prepared to bring her up to speed. I kicked off with telling her about parkrun and going for breakfast with James afterwards.

"I saw James after he left you," informed Molly. "He was very happy to have met up with you and glad that you had time for breakfast this week. I think he still likes you, you know."

"Really?" I asked. "Do you really think he does? He did mention that things weren't going so well with Nat now."

"I think the writing is on the wall for that relationship," remarked Molly. "I don't think either of them are particularly happy. It's a bit awkward if we see them together. Nothing like the fun that the four of us used to have when we went out together."

"Well, that's all well and good. But I have no intention of breaking up anyone's relationship, so I'm not interested in anything other than friendship until he is well and truly single," I explained. "And, I'm not a great believer in looking backwards. If it was going to work out then surely it would have worked out first time around?"

"Well, normally I would agree with you. It's always better to move forwards than revisit the past. However, this is a bit of a different scenario, as you two had only just started dating when Jasmine returned from the US. It made it a very tricky decision for James, and I think if you had been together much longer, he would never have gone back to Jasmine," said Molly. "He clearly regretted his decision fairly quickly, and of course you had moved on with Jack by that point. Sometimes things don't work out because of timing, rather than because of any other reason. And I believe that is the case with you and James."

I chewed my nail thoughtfully.

"Stop chewing your nails," exclaimed Molly. "You know it drives me nuts."

"Sorry, I can't help it," I replied. "It's a sub-conscious habit and I don't even realise that I'm doing it."

Molly's point was very valid. Perhaps there is hope for a rekindle of my romance with James? I suddenly remembered that I hadn't told Molly about Leo yet.

"Oh my god, you wouldn't believe what happened after I left James."

"What happened?" asked Molly.

"I was walking down the road away from the café having just said goodbye to James, when I spotted a familiar face coming the other way. It was Leo."

"Leo? And it's taken until now for you to tell me this?" burst out Molly.

"He wasn't alone," I replied.

"Stop being cryptic. Just tell me what happened." Molly looked frustrated.

"He had his wife and daughter with him. She was only about four years old," I responded.

"Oh my goodness," exclaimed Molly. "Didn't he tell us that he was single?"

"He did indeed," I answered. "He's a total and utter rat. His wife was very pretty, and the daughter just looked angelic. She was clearly his, as she was the spitting image of him. They looked like they were the perfect family. I felt a rather large pang of jealousy to be honest, as well as anger at him."

"Oh no, I'm so sorry. You did really like him didn't you?" commented Molly.

"I did. But what a bastard he is."

"I guess you just have to chalk it up to experience and think of it as a lucky escape," said Molly quietly.

"That's my conclusion too," I replied. "But I will definitely take things slower with any future men that I meet. I'm really annoyed at myself to be honest."

"Well, I wouldn't beat yourself up too much," said Molly. "It's not your fault that you've got terrible taste in men."

I laughed. That broke the tension somewhat, and I felt a bit happier. Sometimes life doesn't go to plan and you have to just do the best that you can.

"When life deals you lemons, sod the lemonade, it's time to make gin and tonic!" I joked.

"Very funny," laughed Molly. "Did you just make that up?"

"I did actually and I'm quite proud of myself," I said.

We continued chatting and I tell Molly all about meeting the seal.

"Good god, I'd have been absolutely terrified," said Molly. "I really hope you're not going back in that river again?"

"Of course I will," I replied. "Although I will make sure that I stay as part of a group next time. I don't think the seal would have approached a group of swimmers. I just got singled out as I happened to end up on my own. The Bluetits group swim every day in the river, and I don't think that has ever happened before, so I doubt it will happen again."

"You are crazy, you really are. There is no way that you would catch me going in a river knowing that a seal might pop up at any time," stated Molly vehemently.

I told Molly that on Monday I would be in touch with the doctors to see if I needed to have a tetanus jab. She said that I must remember to do that and not forget and I promised that I would do so.

We spent the next hour chatting about all sorts of stuff and Molly told me that she was quite excited because she was fairly sure that Harry was thinking about proposing to her. They spent most of their time together, and they had been chatting about the next step in their relationship. They both would like to have a family in the future, and it was probably something that they needed to start seriously thinking about in the not too distant future. I felt really happy for Molly. She deserves her happy ever after. But it does make me feel a little sad that I'm back at the drawing board when it comes to relationships. Still, I feel like I'm a little more knowledgeable now and I had certainly learned some lessons for the future.

Monday soon flew around, and during my lunch hour I called the doctors. It took me about ten minutes to get through, but I finally managed to speak to the receptionist.

"On Saturday I got bitten by a wild animal, and I have no idea if I am up to date on my tetanus vaccination, so I thought I had better check." I provided the lady with my name, address and date of birth so she could look up my records.

"Right, Lily," she replied. "Here we are, I have your records in front of me now. What animal did you get bitten by?"

"It was a seal." There was a silence. A silence that stretched on. "Hello??" I said.

"I'm still here," replied the receptionist. "I was just a bit stunned. How on earth did you get bitten by a seal? I don't think anyone has ever told me that before."

"I was swimming in the river and a seal popped up. It must have swum upstream from the sea. It tried to play with me, but I don't know how to play seal, so it bit me," I explained.

"Wow. That's incredible. If it's a bad bite you should have gone straight to the hospital," stated the receptionist.

"It's not bad at all really, just a puncture of its tooth into my hand really. The seal really wasn't being aggressive, more just playful, but since it has broken the skin, I thought I had better enquire if I needed a tetanus booster," I detailed.

"That is very sensible," responded the receptionist. "If you don't mind holding the line for a couple of minutes, I will quickly consult with one of the doctors. Hold on."

A few minutes later the receptionist confirmed that I should indeed come in for a tetanus booster. But that I could just pop in after work and the nurse on duty would be able to see me. It would only take a couple of minutes, so no need to book an official appointment, and as the bite itself wasn't of concern then there was no need to see a doctor.

Well, that was simple. I would pop in after work and get sorted with the tetanus booster. And then I could forget all about it.

A few hours later, I was seated at the surgery, waiting to see the nurse. As I was reading my Kindle, a man walked in and sat down near to me. Aside from us there were only a handful of older people present. The man was good looking in a boy next door kind of way. He had blonde hair, was tall and slim and had a nice smile. He had clearly come from work as he was wearing a very flattering, well made suit. He looked hot in fact. He seemed familiar but I couldn't place where I had seen him before.

As the minutes passed, I could see that the guy kept checking me out, so I smiled at him. Perhaps he recognised me too.

"How are you doing?" he asked. "Actually, that's a pretty stupid question. You are clearly waiting to see a nurse or a doctor, so it would be logical to assume that something is wrong."

"I'm fine actually," I laughed. "I'm just waiting for a nurse to get a vaccination."

"Oh, I see," said the man. "Snap. Are you going on holiday somewhere exotic?"

"I wish," I replied. "Actually, I got bitten by a seal so I'm having a tetanus booster just in case."

"Well, that's not something that you hear every day," he exclaimed. "How on earth did that happen?"

I filled him in on the seal encounter and then I asked what brought him to the surgery.

"I'm off on holiday to The Gambia, so I'm here for a Yellow Fever vaccination," he responded.

"That sounds interesting. Is it a holiday for pleasure?" I asked.

"Not really," he replied. "Although it will be a fun trip. I volunteer there and the current project is building a school for the kids in a village. I am part of an organisation that do regular projects out there to help make things better for the local communities. So we fundraise for a few months, and then a team of us get sent out to put the money to good use. In the past we've built other things like a doctor's surgery and even a new wing of a hospital."

"That sounds amazing. It must be incredibly rewarding," I commented.

"It is," he replied. "I absolutely love being part of the organisation which is called 'Building Futures in Gambia'. It's incredibly gratifying, but most of all, it gives you a total reality check on life. You realise how lucky we are that we were born and raised in a country with ample food, good education and services and amazing opportunities for everyone who wants them. The world really is our oyster. It's so unfortunate for the kids born in places like The Gambia where there are so few opportunities."

"Isn't Gambia quite a touristy part of the world now?" I asked.

"It is in certain areas," he replied. "However, the more remote areas are incredibly poor. In fact, The Gambia is one of the poorest countries in the world. The tourism industry there does of course bring in money, but it doesn't seem to get to the people that actually need it. But at Building Futures in Gambia, we try to make a difference. I have personally been visiting regularly for the past decade, so I know a lot of the local people in the areas that we work. They are so grateful for the help that we provide them. We make a real impact on their lives."

"That's truly amazing," I responded. "What is your name?"

"Sorry, that's rather rude of me. My name is George," he replied. "How about you?"

"I'm Lily," I said with a smile. I held out my hand and he shook it.

"It's really good to meet you Lily. You seem like a really interesting person," said George. "In fact, you look familiar to me."

"I thought the same," I replied. I wracked my brains. I had one of those lightbulb moments. "You don't happen to have two black labradors do you?"

"Aha, that's it," George replied. "I don't, but my friend does, and I was walking them recently when he was away. That was your picnic that they disrupted wasn't it?"

At that, I heard my name being called. A nurse carrying a clipboard entered the room, so I stood up and then hesitated, turning back to George.

"It was great to meet you again," I responded.

As I turn to go, I heard George say something. I turned back.

"Wait, hold on," he said fumbling in his rucksack. "Take this." George handed me a business card.

"Give me a call, Lily," he said. "Perhaps we could meet up sometime."

"I will," I agreed. "Bye for now."

I followed the nurse who walked me down the corridor to a small consulting room. The nurse expertly asked me a few questions, checked my vitals and then administered the tetanus vaccination. She did it so skilfully that I didn't even realise she had finished. I literally didn't even feel the needle.

"All sorted for you," she said smiling.

"Thank you very much," I replied. "Enjoy the rest of your day."

As I headed towards the exit of the building, I looked into the waiting room, but George was no longer there. He must have been called in to one of the other consulting rooms. Pleased to have got the vaccination out of the way, I headed home, wondering if Molly might be in tonight.

As I wandered into the kitchen, I heard the clink of a wine bottle. Molly was indeed home and she was in the process of pouring two glasses of wine. She handed one to me and asked me if I had got hold of the doctors. I explained that I had been to the surgery for a booster from one of the nurses.

"And, interestingly, I met a man in the waiting room," I stated.

"Ooh, tell me more, Lily," Molly said with a smirk.

"Well, he was fit, blonde, pretty good looking and called George. He was also there for a vaccination, although his was for yellow fever because he's going to The Gambia in a few weeks to help build a school," I disclosed.

"Well, that's pretty commendable," she remarked.

I fished the business card out of my pocket. I had actually nearly forgotten about it, and hadn't looked at it at all yet.

"Well, he works for Riley Construction," I read out. "It says here that he's a Director."

"Well, that's pretty high up then. How old was he?" Molly asked.

"I'm not sure, but I would guess a similar age to me," I replied. "He asked me to message him. Do you think I should send a message to him now or wait a day or two?"

"Well, seeing as he's disappearing to Gambia soon, you might as well message him now," Molly suggested. "You did check that he wasn't wearing a wedding ring, right?"

"Haha, very funny. I won't make that mistake again," I laughed. "He didn't have a wedding ring on anyway. And I did check very carefully for a dent on the ring finger this time."

"Well, that's good to know. Why don't you give him a Google seeing as you know his full name this time?" suggested Molly.

"That's a great idea. Thanks Molly," I replied.

I proceeded to bring Molly up to date on my initial meeting with George and the two labradors.

"What a coincidence," Molly said.

I pulled out my phone and put George Riley into the search engine. A number of different results came up. There were a few Facebook profiles that were of that name, and there were about four different articles about Building Futures in Gambia. I had a quick look on Facebook and there was a profile for him with pictures, clearly of him helping out at various building projects. I then clicked into one of the newspaper articles in which he was mentioned. It seemed his dad, Liam Riley, is the Managing Director of Riley Construction, and George has worked his way up in the firm since he graduated from Liverpool University. According to the article, George is 32 years old. His Facebook profile says that he is single. Well, that's a start at least.

I handed the phone over to Molly so that she could have a look. She took the phone and whistled.

"My, he's hot property," she exclaimed. "He is very nice looking indeed. And obviously from a good background and clearly has a nice, caring nature."

"He did appear to have lots of empathy. It was evident how much he cares about the work that he gets involved with in Gambia," I stated.

"He sounds too good to be true," replied Molly.

"I think I deserve a break after the last disaster with Leo."

"Indeed you do. You've not really had much luck recently what with Jack turning into a bastard and Leo being a rat. You deserve a nice man to come along," said Molly.

"Right, I'm going to message him then," I confirmed.

I think hard about what to say and after a few attempts, Molly and I decide that this is the best message that we can come up with:

It was a pleasure to meet you today. How long is it until you go to Gambia?

I hit the send button, and then place my mobile on the table in front of us. I pick up my wine glass and take a sip.

"I hate waiting for someone to call or message. It's a nightmare. You just want to keep picking up the phone to see if they have responded," I said.

"Lily, you need to learn to be patient, all in good time," smiled Molly.

"It's alright for you, you are all loved up and things are getting serious between you and Harry," I replied. "Honestly, I'm happy for you. But I really could do with finding someone for myself. I just seem to keep messing things up. Maybe I'm destined to be forever single."

"Rubbish Lily. Don't get all despondent on me now. Mr Right will come along soon, don't you worry. Or perhaps we should say Mr Riley?"

"I don't know about Mr Right, I'm thinking I need Mr Right Now," I mused.

Molly burst out laughing. "Honestly, Lily. You crack me up. You really need to take a chill pill. Good things will come, you'll see. Just have faith."

As I took a sip of my wine, there was a ding from my phone.

"Ooh, I think he's replied already." I excitedly grabbed for my phone and managed to spill some of the wine down my top in the process. "God, I'm so clumsy!" I stated.

I flick the cover of the phone over and hold it up for face recognition.

Good to meet you too Lily. I'm leaving in just over two weeks. Would you like to meet for a drink on Thursday night? George

"He wants to meet up Thursday night. Do you think I should say yes, or is that a bit keen?" I asked.

"Crack on, Lily. If he's off soon you might as well make the most of the time that you have left," suggested Molly.

That sounds ideal. When and where?

A few more messages either way confirmed the time and place to meet. It was a nice pub within walking distance (assuming you like a good walk) so I'd not have to worry about driving. I wasn't sure if we would be eating, as the pub has a good reputation, so I decided that I would have a snack before I go. That way, it wouldn't matter if we ate or not.

Chapter 12

Thankfully it was dry and sunny on Thursday night, so I had a very enjoyable forty-five minute walk to the pub in the sunshine. Molly came with me, just because she fancied a nice walk. I think she wanted to check out George really, after what she's heard and read about him.

I arrived fifteen minutes early, so I bought myself a cider and sat in the beer garden. Many of the tables were already taken, but I managed to find one that was still bathed in sunlight. Molly had opted to have a quick drink inside, not wanting to gatecrash my date. So I'd left her supping on a white wine at the bar. She'd get to see George before I did, assuming of course that he turned up. I often get a little paranoid that if I arranged to meet someone for a date they might just not turn up. It's never happened to me yet – but I'd be mortified if it did. Still, at least if it happened today, I had Molly here, so I wouldn't have to look like an idiot for too long.

However, panic over. I saw George pop his head out of the door and wave at me. He raised his hand in a drinking gesture, and I lifted up my cider to show him that I've already got one thank you. He mouthed 'back in a sec' at me and headed inside to the bar.

A few minutes later he was back with a pint of lager, and he walked straight up for an air kiss on both cheeks. What a polite gentleman he was.

"Lily, you look gorgeous," George stated with a broad smile. "Here, I got these for you."

He hands over a bunch of daffodils, freshly picked, both yellow and white.

"They are beautiful, but I hope you didn't steal them from someone's garden," I asked.

"Of course not, I just walked past loads of them along the towpath of the river. I would never steal from someone's garden," he replied.

"Glad to hear it," I responded with a smile.

We chatted lightly for a few minutes about the last few days and what we had been up to. I was keen to find out more about George's Gambian adventure, so I lost no time in asking about it.

"I've actually been every year for much of the last decade. Aside from the Covid years of course. We've been involved with so many different projects and have really contributed to the building of a community for the Gambian people," said George.

"That's amazing," I exclaimed. "I really am in awe of the dedication that you show."

"I've raised over £25,000 personally over the last three years as well. And that money goes towards building supplies for our projects," he enlightened me.

"Wow, that's a lot of money. How did you raise that much? I find fundraising really hard – it seems to be the same people that you are asking for donations all the time," I said.

"I have done quite a few crazy stunts to raise money. And I plan and execute events a lot of the time – like a dinner dance. Or a barn dance. Events that people will pay to attend. I did an auction of promises donated from local companies – that was extremely fruitful and raised over £9,000 in one go," explained George.

"That's so commendable. You must be so proud. How long will you be away for?" I asked.

"I am truly proud. Although I'm part of a great team. There are around 20 of us that work together to raise money, and then probably 8 or 9 of us take a trip each year to work on the live projects. I'm going for eight weeks this time, which will give us a chance to get the majority of the structural work for the school completed. So then, it will really only be the little jobs, which a lot of the locals will be able to undertake," responded George.

As well as being incredibly attracted to George, I felt really excited that I had finally met a truly good person. Who is single, works hard, looks after himself and loves to volunteer. These are all amazing qualities that I would wish for in my partner.

As I had those thoughts, I saw Molly poke her head out of the doorway from the bar. She put her thumbs up and then waved. She clearly approved of George and was heading home. I smiled an acknowledgement to her.

George and I continued to talk about Gambia. It's kind of typical that I have met him just as he's about to disappear for a couple of months, however, eight weeks would fly by. It's nothing in the grand scheme of things. If it's meant to be, it will work out somehow. Eventually, he turns the conversation around, and asked me about wild swimming.

"I've only been doing it for the past few weeks, but I absolutely love it. I've met some fabulous people and I'm really enjoying getting to know a new group of people," I explained.

"Are you going to stop in the winter time when it gets very cold?" asked George.

"No, I'm planning on swimming all year round if I can. That's the intention anyway. Some of the ladies swear that the benefits are magnified as the water gets colder," I said.

"What are the key benefits?" asked George.

"Well, the health benefits are scientifically proven. The cold water helps reduce inflammation in the body, it helps regulate thermal control of the body, it can reduce pain, it helps lower blood pressure and more. Then, and probably more importantly to me, are the wellbeing benefits. You feel amazing afterwards. You feel in touch with nature. You feel part of a community. You embrace the serenity, and you feel at peace with the world. You can reduce your concerns and anxiety, you can relieve depression and it certainly brings joy into your life," I stated.

"Wow, I had no idea," replied George. "That's amazing. Maybe I'm missing out. I think I should come with you sometime."

"You'd be very welcome. The Bluetits do have some male members and you'd be able to join me anytime that you would like."

"That sounds great, I might just take you up on that," said George. "That's a great name for a wild swimming group."

I explained to George the background about the Bluetits. The fact that they are an international organisation with local groups throughout the UK and many other countries. George seems equally as impressed with the Bluetits as I am with the Gambian Futures organisation.

The rest of the evening passed extremely pleasantly. We had a great time together chatting, laughing and just generally getting to know each other. I didn't even remember to feel hungry, despite only eating some crackers and cheese. George bought me a second pint whilst he drank a Guinness 0% as he was driving. He offered me a lift home which I gratefully accepted as it meant that we could stay talking for longer. I wouldn't have wanted to walk home in the dark on my own.

At the end of the evening, George dropped me outside my house. He drove a blue BMW car which was rather sporty and nice. He clearly had money behind him, although didn't have a pretentious bone in his body. He truly seemed like a genuinely nice person. As he pulled up, he stopped the car, jumped out and walked swiftly around to hold my door as I stepped out of the car. What an absolute gentleman he was. His manners were impeccable, which is quite rare but very refreshing. He took hold of my hand and gave me a quick peck on the lips.

"I'll call you tomorrow," he confirmed. "Perhaps we can get together this weekend?"

"That sounds great," I agreed. "I'd very much like to see you again."

At that, I bid him goodnight and I headed inside. Molly had gone back to Harry's, so I was on my own. But I did remember to message her and confirm that I was home, safe and alone. I also sent a message to George.

Thank you for the lift home and a lovely evening. I will look forward to seeing you at the weekend.

x

Half an hour later I got a very short reply which just said:

Ditto

G xxxx

As I drifted off to sleep later that night, a smile crept on my lips. I must not overthink things. But I was excited to see where this fledgling relationship was going to go.

Chapter 13

On Friday evening I had a text exchange with George. He wanted to take me out for the day on Saturday. I asked what he wanted to do, and he said that ideally, he'd like to have kept it as a surprise, but realistically that wasn't feasible as I needed to know what we were going to do so that I could be prepared. He said that he was going to take me to an indoor ski centre which had artificial snow.

I'm really excited about that as I have always wanted to ski indoors. I once saw one at Milton Keynes when I was on a day trip for an indoor skydive experience, but I haven't had a chance to try it out. I have had a couple of ski holidays, so I know the basics of how to ski, but I'm definitely no expert, and I've not been for a couple of years, so it would be really nice to refresh on my ski technique.

I spent a couple of hours on Friday evening digging out salopettes, gloves, ski jacket, helmet and goggles. It took me a while as I wasn't sure what I had done with my kit. I eventually found everything in a suitcase in the loft at mum's house.

Saturday morning, George arrived promptly at 8am to collect me. I would of course miss parkrun this week but was happy to forgo it on this occasion. I was ready and waiting as he pulled up to the kerb outside the house and as I walked over to him, he jumped out to help me put my things in the boot and give me a kiss. This time he went for a kiss on the lips which felt rather nice.

Being the utmost gentleman, George opened the car door for me and held it while I sat down and got settled. He then headed round to the driver's seat and off we went. It turned out that we were going to the Milton Keynes centre that I had once seen. It was a good couple of hours drive from home, so I settled in for the journey, chatting contentedly.

"Have you eaten breakfast?" asked George.

"No, I haven't. I'm actually quite hungry," I replied.

"I know an amazing place for breakfast just before we get on the dual carriageway that takes us most of the way to Milton Keynes," he suggested.

"That sounds ideal, let's do it," was my reply.

Twenty minutes later we pulled up to a café called 'Broken Eggs'. It looked perfect as it was clean, shiny and busy. That's always a good sign that the food is good. We sat down and perused the menu. Shortly afterwards, a very pretty waitress sashayed over with a big beaming smile on her face.

"Hello, little Bruv," said the waitress.

"This is your sister?" I exclaimed. "You didn't tell me that your sister worked here."

"Yes, Lily meet Anna. Anna meet Lily," replied George.

I offered my hand to Anna, and she took it with a firm grasp and gave me a convincing shake.

"It's really good to meet you Lily," said Anna. "I'd love to say that I'd heard all about you, but he's certainly kept you quiet."

"Well, we only met a few days ago," I replied with a laugh.

"I haven't spoken to you since meeting Lily to bring you up to speed, Sis," said George. "We are off to Milton Keynes so I thought it would be a good opportunity for the two of you to meet."

"Are you on a shopping trip?" asked Anna. "I didn't think you were that keen on shopping George?"

"I'm not keen on shopping either," I said to Anna. "We are off to the indoor ski centre."

"Oh, that's awesome," said Anna. "You will have a fabulous time. It's really fun. I go regularly when I'm not working."

"I've not been before," I explained. "But I have had a couple of skiing holidays in the past so I know the basics."

"That's good," replied Anna. "Because you have to book a lesson if you are a beginner. They won't let you out on the slope unless you know the basics."

"I can hold my own," I replied. "And George has offered to help me as he is a more experienced skier than I am."

"Yes, George is pretty decent. He'll be able to make sure that you get the best out of the day," said Anna.

At that, Anna asked what we wanted to eat. I ordered Eggs Benedict and George ordered a Full English breakfast. Anna wandered off after jotting our order down, and I could see her talking to the staff in the kitchen.

We started chatting about ski holidays that we had had in the past. I have been once to the Three Valleys in France, and once to Arc 2000. Conversely, George has skied in lots of places including Whistler, Canada as well as various places in Europe.

"I'm happy on blue runs, and I can tenuously tackle the easier red runs," I explained to George when he asks what standard I am.

"That's good," he said. "That means that you have the basics in place, and then it's just a case of growing in confidence and fine-tuning your skills. I can help you improve a little even just in a day like today."

I felt really excited to be doing something fun like this, with an incredible person like George. I might have only known him a few days, but I felt really comfortable with him, I enjoyed his company, and he is very easy on the eye.

Our breakfast soon arrived and it looked absolutely delicious. I'm not sure whether we got special treatment, or if it's that good for everyone, but it was truly sensational and there was plenty of it. We were both hungry and tucked in well, so the conversation became limited. There was a really easy atmosphere between us though. There were no awkward silences, and I didn't once feel like I needed to find something to say.

We'd soon cleared out plates and it was time to get back on the road. We bid farewell to Anna, and she gave us both a big hug and made us promise to meet up again soon. We headed out to the car and were soon back on our journey.

"That was such a great breakfast, and it was lovely to meet Anna, she's really nice" I commented.

"She is great," agreed George. "I don't see her as often as I like but only because we are both such busy people. We get on fabulously when we do see each other."

"How much older is she?" I asked.

"Anna is thirty-five and I am thirty-two," replied George. "So she's three years older than I am."

"Do you have any other siblings?" I questioned.

"No, it's just the two of us," confirmed George.

We continued chatting comfortably, talking about skiing and our families. In what felt like no time at all, we were pulling up outside the massive building that housed the ski centre on the outskirts of Milton Keynes.

As we walked from the car into the centre, I could feel George bump his arm into mine a couple of times. It felt like there were sparks flying between us, and I was very acutely aware of the chemistry building up. There was no doubt that we were both attracted to each other. Once we headed through the doors into the interior of the centre, it was quite busy, so George took hold of my hand. It felt nice and I relished the closeness that was developing between us. It was exciting and made me want more from him.

Initially it was a little confusing as there were lots of people, and there seemed to be many shops, restaurants and different activities to do. I saw signs for the sky dive experience which I had taken part in a couple of years ago. We followed the throng of people hoping to find a sign for the ski centre, and a few minutes later we were successful. We'd actually entered the building at the opposite end to the ski slope, thus being a bit disorientated.

The centre itself was very impressive. There was so much to do, as well as a myriad of shops and restaurants. We certainly wouldn't be leaving hungry or thirsty, although right now I was still full up from the delicious breakfast. We headed straight to the ski area and checked in at the reception desk. We were guided towards the ski and ski boot hire area and a very helpful man got us all kitted out. Then we headed towards the slope and the lift situated at the bottom of it.

The lift is a drag lift with a large button on the end of a pole which you put between your legs, and you then get towed up the slope. I had used these types of drag lifts all the time when I was on my ski holidays, so I wasn't remotely apprehensive. Perhaps that was where I went wrong. George gestured for me to go first, so I waited in line and then grabbed the next button that was free. I popped it between my legs and waited for the small jolt that you usually feel as you start your climb up the slope. The next thing I realised is that I was only stood on one ski, I was totally off balance and I seemed to be heading off at a tangent to all the other people being dragged up the slope. I then managed to cross my skis in front of me, and so they ground to a halt whilst my upper body kept being pulled up the slope. I end up in a big, unruly heap, spun around facing back down the slope with one ski up, one crossed over and George heading towards me on the next button. It was time to surrender, and as I let go the button pinged upwards away from me and I start to slide in a very unladylike sprawl towards George with skis going in all directions.

I could see that George was trying desperately hard not to laugh. He let go of the lift and used his momentum to ski over to me and help me up. He first pulled me clear of the lift so that I was not obstructing the next person. I could see that all the people in the queue behind us were in hysterics and I know that I'm bright red. I felt so stupid. So much for holding my own. I can't even use the lift competently.

"Oh my god, I'm mortified," I stated to George.

"Seriously, don't worry," responded George. "It's just a rookie mistake. You were balanced on one ski as the drag lift caught you, so you just got pulled over. We've all done it."

"Really?" I asked. "You've done that too?"

"Well, of sorts, yes," said George. "And much worse too, so don't stress about it."

At that, George held out his hands to pull me up. He then set about collecting my loose ski and helped me step my ski boot back into it.

"There we are," said George. "No harm done. Shall we go for take two?"

"Yes," I replied. "I will ensure I'm concentrating this time."

We headed back to the queue at the bottom of the lift for another go. Unfortunately, I could see one of the staff heading towards us. No doubt I would get quizzed or maybe even banned from the slope.

"Have you skied before?" asked the high-viz snow steward.

"Yes," I sighed. "Believe it or not, I can actually ski. I just had a brain lapse and wasn't concentrating."

"Well, have another go then. If you can't manage the lift you will need to book a lesson with us. We can't have beginners on these slopes unless they have one of our instructors with them," replied the steward.

"It's fine," I responded with a confidence I wasn't really feeling.

As I waited for my turn, George put his arm around me and gave me a hug.

"Is it too early to say that it was really quite funny?" he asked.

"Yes, it's definitely too early," I replied with a wry smile. George held me against his side and gave me a squeeze.

"Right, come on. Let's go again," encouraged George with a smile.

This time I made sure that my skis were straight out in front of me, and that my weight was balanced equally over them. I turned slightly to watch for the button to reach level with me, before I took hold of it and carefully popped it between my legs. I leaned back slightly waiting for the initial tug.

Yes. Thank goodness. This time things went to plan, and I safely began the upward journey pulled along by the button lift. I heard George cheering behind me, and I felt much happier.

"Jump off at the first exit," called George.

As we reached level with the first exit ramp, I took hold of the button and removed it from between my legs. I let go and concentrated on sliding down the exit ramp without falling over. I navigated successfully to a fence at the side of the main slope.

"Well done, Lily," said George. "That went well."

"Thank goodness," I mumbled. "I was mortified at making a complete tit of myself."

"It really wasn't that bad," said George kindly.

"Well, at least I've made it to the main slope this time," I smiled. I couldn't help but smile at George. He is so compassionate and nice.

"So, let's head down the slope nice and steadily. Use all the width of the slope and don't forget to turn at each end to control your speed. Don't try to be too fast until you have got back into it," suggested George.

I left the safety of the fence and made sure that I had my poles ready and I was off. I traversed across the slope, trying to remember what I had been taught during ski school. I felt a little bit wobbly, but actually as I gained a little more momentum it felt better, and I felt more balanced. As I progressed well across the slope it was time to try a turn. I tried to remember to lighten my weight as the skis started to turn, and make sure that I landed after the turn back on my downhill ski.

On that first turn, I nearly caught an edge, and remembered to make sure my weight was moved off the upper ski throughout the turn. I successfully navigated the first turn, albeit with a bit of a wobble and started to traverse back towards the lift.

As I approached the edge of the slope there was a group of people helping up someone that had fallen over. I was in two minds to go past them and turn in the small space left before the lift, or turn before them. It seemed prudent to take the safer option, so I turned before reaching them, ensuring that I didn't crash into them or the lone ski and pole that had been dropped by the stricken skier.

The second turn was much smoother than the first and I was soon traversing back across the slope. The next three turns became a little smoother and slicker as my memory of the technique and feel started to return. With the turns completed, a little of my previous confidence trickled back. I completed the slope and finished back at the drag lift ready to go again. With a big, beaming smile on my face I looked back to see that George had stopped to help the stricken skier. He had collected up the abandoned ski and pole and was handing them back. That was nice of him to help.

Once he was able, he set off down the remainder of the slope and I was able to watch him ski effortlessly in just two turns back down to me. He looked like he owned the slope. He looked so professional compared to everyone else present. As he pulled up next to me with a flourish, he congratulated me on my ever-improving skiing.

"You did great, Lily" enthused George. "You looked like you were getting more confident with every turn."

"I did feel like I could remember some of the technique that I was previously taught. I guess it's a bit like riding a bike, it's a skill that once mastered will stay with you, even if you haven't skied for a while," I said.

"That's right," agreed George. "It comes back incredibly quickly if you've not skied for some time. Are you ready to go again? We could go up another level this time, there are fewer people up there and the slope isn't any steeper or more difficult."

"Yes, let's do that. I'll get a bit more time to ski then," I said.

The lift this time seemed pretty easy in comparison, and in fact over the next half an hour or so, we enjoyed several trips up and down the slope. I could see that it was really easy for George, but he stayed with me, gave me a few pointers, and generally added to my confidence by being nearby.

"Shall we head to the top this time?" suggested George.

"It looks much steeper towards the top," I worried. "Do you think I will be ok?"

"You'll be absolutely fine. It's actually easier to turn when the gradient is a little steeper and you seem totally in control at the moment. I think it will do you good, and you will get a better feeling from a longer ski," said George.

"Right, ok," I replied. "Let's do it."

This time, instead of leaving the drag lift at the second ramp exit, we stayed on it to the very top of the slope. I started to get a little nervous as I felt the gradient become much steeper. But George reassured me that I am competent enough to ski it.

"You go first, then if you do have any difficulties I can help," instructed George.

At least this part of the slope was fairly clear of other people. I set off traversing across the steepest part of the slope. As I approached my first turning point, I had a little wobble of confidence. I wasn't sure now if I could do this.

As I attempted my first turn, I didn't lighten my weight enough, and I just caught my upper ski. I had an extremely precarious wobble although I did manage to stay upright, but now I was starting to gain speed and was heading straight down the slope.

I was getting faster and faster and I could hear George shouting at me.

"Turn, Lily. Turn."

I had a moment of panic because I was now going so fast that I was scared to attempt a turn. But I was going to have to do something because right now I was heading far too fast straight down the slope towards a group of people. Time to pull myself together and take charge.

I ensured this time that I leaned to the right and had my weight almost completely on my right hand ski and I started to turn towards the left. I just had to wait and give the ski time to turn, and then use the traversing of the slope to slow down. Finally, I was starting to regain some control, the speed was falling away and I no longer felt like I was going to crash. Coming up to the next turning point, the speed had now levelled off and I felt back in control. I executed a fairly good turn this time and was able to competently ski the remaining slope in about three turns.

As I reached the fence at the bottom of the slope, I was glad to come to a stop. I turned around to watch George join me with a flourish.

"Well done, Lily," complimented George. "That was a good save. I thought you had lost it at one point, but you managed to regain control and save yourself."

"That was very close," I stuttered. "I had a bit of a wobble when I caught my ski, and then I froze a little bit as I ended up going so fast. I was pleased to be able to recover however and ski the remaining elements of the slope successfully."

"I think it probably felt a lot worse than it looked," stated George. "I could see that you had lost your balance, and then gained too much speed, but after a few seconds you seemed to cope well with it. I'm quite impressed, Lily.

You did well. The main thing is not to panic and to use the slope to help control your speed."

"Thanks," I replied. "I could do with a rest now."

"Well, our slot is coming to an end in any case. We've maybe got time for one more ski, unless you would rather get a coffee now?" asked George.

"I think I'm done. My legs are starting to feel rather jelly like, and I'm quite cold too now. A cup of tea sounds like a great plan," I confirmed. "Why don't you head up and have a final ski while I get rid of my ski boots, skis and poles?"

"Are you sure you wouldn't mind?" asked George.

"Of course not, please go. In fact, I'll wait just in that area over there where it's warmer, but I can still see you. I'd like to watch you do your final run," I suggested.

George agreed and headed off to the lift for the final run. I went over to the benches in the kit change area and unclipped my boots from the skis. I then took off my ski boots which felt amazing. To be honest, they weren't fitting me that well, but as we were only doing a single session, by the time I had figured out they didn't fit me very well it seemed pointless to change. It was so nice to release my feet from the confines of the boot.

By the time I had handed my skis, boots and poles back to the staff member, George had reached the very top of the slope. I sat down in a warm, heated area and watched as he skied effortlessly down the slope. He was making a few sweeping turns, keeping up a really good momentum and looking like a total professional. He almost looked lazy, like he wasn't doing anything, but I knew that he just had really good technique. It was interesting to watch, and George looked so much better than anyone else on the slope. I felt very proud to be with him.

In no time at all, George had reached the bottom of the slope. He unclipped from his skis and headed into the kit change area to hand things back. He'd told me that he had his own skis but it was just as easy to use those belonging to the centre, rather than digging out his own. A few minutes later we were sitting in the next door coffee shop, and George went to the counter to get himself a latte and a tea for me. It was nice to warm up. The air temperature on the slopes was minus five degrees, so I was grateful of the nice warm coffee shop and the cup of tea to wrap my hands around.

Whilst George was collecting our drinks, I reflected on my performance on the ski slope. Despite the poor start, I think I did ok. It definitely feels harder than skiing on real snow in the mountains, and the fact that the ski slope is quite short means that you don't get many turns per run. But, I really enjoyed it and felt like I improved a lot during the session. George was a great instructor. Helping me with tips and pointers but not overloading me. He was very encouraging and enthusiastic. Overall, I had thoroughly enjoyed the morning. It was surprising quite how tired I felt now though. In comparison to a ski holiday, where you would probably ski for three hours straight, have lunch, and then ski for a couple more hours, we had only skied for a total of an hour and a half. And I felt shattered.

"Here you are, Lily," said George as he put the drinks down on the table. "I got you a chocolate brownie as well. I hope that was a good choice for you?"

"My favourite," I confirmed. "That is the perfect choice and just what I need. I feel really tired now - I could do with a sugar boost."

"It's hard work," said George. "You don't get a rest when you are using drag lifts, and the runs are quite short on the indoor slopes, so it's quite physically demanding. In the mountains a lot of the lifts are chair lifts, so you get a good long rest on those."

"You're right," I agreed. "I hadn't thought of that."

George settled down next to me, and then slipped an arm around my waist. I snuggled into his shoulder. I felt really happy. I felt tired. I felt content. If I was a cat, I would be purring right now.

We spent the next thirty minutes drinking, chatting, eating our respective chocolate brownies and discussing the skiing. I felt more or less happy with the session, other than the total shambles I made of the lift at the beginning. I had really enjoyed George's company. He truly was a good man.

Afterwards, we had a wander through the centre, and then watched a few people do the indoor skydive. George hadn't seen it before, so he was keen to take a look. It was nice for me to be the experienced one this time and explain what it's like. The skydive centre was fully booked for the day, so we didn't have the option to have a go ourselves, but it was nice to watch a few other people do it. And then it was time to leave. We headed back to the car, with a head full of happy memories.

Chapter 14

A few hours later, I was sitting at the kitchen table with Molly, detailing the fabulous morning with George. We had a glass of wine each and were getting ready to go out for the evening. We'd arranged to go for dinner together with George and Harry. Molly was excited to meet George properly as she had heard so much about him. Of course, she had seen him from a distance, but not yet talked to him. We were going to eat at the same restaurant that we'd gone to for my 30th birthday last year. It's a steakhouse with a fabulous reputation.

As we both wanted to drink this evening, we decided to get an Uber to the restaurant, so that had been ordered and was on its way. We'd had a couple of changes of clothes, and I had settled on a check shirt with jeans and short boots. My look had a hint of cowgirl meets city, and Molly had worn a pretty summery dress as she likes to.

We arrived at the restaurant a few minutes early, so we were the first to be shown to our table. We were seated at a table, laid for six, in the middle of the restaurant with a good view of everyone around us. I chose a seat facing the entrance so that I could easily spot when George arrived. When the waitress came around, Molly ordered a bottle of Prosecco for us to share. She asked the waitress to bring four glasses in case George and Harry wanted some too.

The door to the restaurant opened and in walked a couple, hand in hand. I glanced over briefly, thinking that I recognised them. It was James and Nat. I hadn't actually met Nat before, but I assumed that it was her. James spoke to the host, and the host picked up some menus and led James and Nat across to us.

"Evening Molly, Evening Lily. How are you both?" James asked.

"I'm good thanks," replied Molly. "I didn't realise you were joining us this evening."

"It's all been a bit last minute," said James. "When Harry told me that you were all coming here tonight, we thought we'd tag along. Harry called the restaurant and changed the booking to 6 people. I hope that's ok with you both?"

"Fine with me," I said, and Molly also nodded her approval.

"Lily, I don't think you've met Nat before," said James. "Nat, this is Lily, Lily this is Nat."

I smiled at Nat and stood up to accept a brief hug and air kiss from her. Nat then gave Molly a warm hug. They of course knew each other well. Molly had never really told me that much about Nat, but they seemed on friendly terms. James also walked around the table to give me a hug, and then he pulled out a chair for Nat to sit on, before sitting across from me.

"Where's Harry?" I asked.

"He's just parking the car," replied James. "He's putting it into the staff section of the car park so that it can be left overnight and he can have some drinks."

"That sounds sensible," I commented.

"Nat, you are welcome to join us in drinking the Prosecco if you wish," I offered. Nat gracefully accepted and I passed her one of the flutes. James ordered himself and Harry a lager.

"Where's your fella?" asked James.

"He'll be here shortly," I replied.

As I looked over, I could see the restaurant door opening again and in walked Harry and a few steps behind him was George. Harry had immediately spotted us, and I could see George having a quiet word with the host. As he looked around the restaurant, I stood up and waved, and he acknowledged my greeting and started weaving his way towards us.

George walked up to our table, and as I stood, he took my hands and gave me a kiss on the lips.

"You look beautiful, Lily," he commented. "It's great to see you again."

"Likewise," I replied. "I'm excited for you to meet my friends."

At that, I turned to the others and introduced George to them. He shook hands with Harry and then James, and gave a brief air kiss to Nat and Molly.

"I recognise you from the bar other night," George said to Molly.

"I was just making sure that you arrived, and checked you out on behalf of Lily," laughed Molly.

"Well, I hope that I got your approval," he responded.

George also ordered a lager and sat next to me. Everyone settled down into their seats and started chatting. I had George on one side of me and Harry on the other. James and Nat were across the other side, and Molly was next to Harry.

"I heard that you had a brilliant time at the indoor ski centre this morning," commented Molly to George.

"We had a great day," responded George. "Aside from an early unscheduled dismount off the drag lift, Lily skied really well and we had a lot of fun."

"Oh dear," said Molly. "You kept that quiet Lily!"

"Well, it was a bit mortifying to be honest," I replied. "But everything went pretty well after that, so all things considered I wasn't that bothered."

"I think you did great Lily," commented George. "I was really proud of you." He took hold of my hand and squeezed it, and then picked up his pint. "In fact, I'd like to make a toast. To new beginnings."

"To new beginnings," chanted everyone, raising their glasses for a clink.

I noticed Nat turn to look at James with a scowl on her face. The two of them had a whispered discussion that looked a little unpleasant, and then I could see Nat almost turn her back on James and she stared into her Prosecco glass. She picked up the bottle, but as it was empty, she scowled again and then looked around the room to catch the eye one of the waitresses. She held up the Prosecco bottle and the waitress nodded that she would bring a new one over.

The rest of the group perused the menu, and the waitress soon came over with a new bottle of Prosecco. She opened that, topped up Nat's glass, and then deposited the bottle in the cooler that had been provided. She then whipped out a pen and her order pad.

Everyone ordered, and it was a fairly simple order all round as everyone chose sirloin steaks. Nat however chose a fillet steak, then had a number of questions about whether it came with sauce, if the sauce was on the side or on the steak, what salad it came with and what dressing was available. I could see that James had a very pained expression on his face, and Harry looked awkward as well. Finally, Nat was done with her order, and the group resumed talking. We'd moved on to what everyone else had done today, and James and Harry filled us in on their day which consisted of a game of squash followed by a long bike ride. James explained that he was training for a triathlon later in the year, so he was out on his bike for a couple of hours most weekends. Unfortunately, today he'd had a puncture, and had some issues dealing with it on the side of the road, so he started discussing the pros and cons of tubeless tyres with Harry. Nat was looking very detached, ignoring everyone and downing her Prosecco at an impressive rate.

I studied Nat closely, without trying to be too obvious. She was a pretty woman, but with a permanent scowl on her face, she wasn't attractive at all. I was surprised that James was with her, because he was such a nice man. He seemed very tolerant of her behaviour, although was definitely looking a little embarrassed. Other than the initial whispered conversation, Nat and James hadn't chatted together at all, and it was obvious that their relationship was not going well.

After a little wait, our food arrived, and it looked very impressive. As the meals were dished out, another bottle of Prosecco and some lagers were ordered. Molly and I were still on our second glass of Prosecco and Nat had caned the rest of it. I asked for a jug of water to be provided, and that duly turned up with plenty of ice, some lemon and some water glasses. I dished out the water to everyone except Nat as she rudely pushed the glass away when I offered it to her.

The chatter resumed quietly as we all tucked into our meals. I could see that Nat wasn't really eating much, she seemed to be pushing the food around her plate and frowning. Finally, I could see that she gestured to a waitress who came over with a big smile on her face.

"This is not acceptable," snapped Nat to the waitress.

"I'm so sorry, what seems to be the issue?" the waitress responded.

"The sauce is revolting, and it's cold. And I asked for it to be provided on the side, not on the steak itself. I can't eat this. It will have to go back to the kitchen," complained Nat.

I am fairly sure that I could remember Nat specifying that she wanted the sauce on the steak, not on the side. I do get bothered by people who complain about ridiculous things. It all ends up in the same place anyway, so is there really any need to kick up a fuss?

"I'm so sorry madam," replied the waitress politely. "I will send it back to the kitchen."

The waitress picked up the plate and returned to the kitchen. James turned to Nat and I could see him talking quietly to her, and she snapped back at him. On the other side I could see Harry turn to Molly, rolling his eyes, making Molly laugh. Harry clearly had the same opinion as myself, and I could see that Harry didn't like Nat very much.

Nat continued to stare at the table, drinking her Prosecco. The rest of us felt rather awkward, and conversation was a little stilted for a few moments. I looked at George, and he smiled kindly at me, then reached for my hand and gave it a squeeze. Nat suddenly stood up, grabbed her bag and coat and walked towards the exit of the restaurant.

"What's going on James?" asked Harry.

"Nat is having a strop," replied James. "She didn't really want to come, but she's made no effort at all and I think she had a few glasses of wine before we came out. So now she's just being a right pain in the arse. I really can't be doing with this type of behaviour."

"She certainly can be rather moody," replied Harry. "What went wrong? She didn't used to be like this."

"I have no idea," said James. "She just seemed to gradually change over time, and now she is just grumpy and stroppy. I'd better go find her and see if she is staying or going home."

James stood up and headed for the exit. The waitress came back carrying a new plate of steak and chips with the sauce on the side this time.

"What's going on?" she asked. "Has the lady left?"

"I don't know," replied Harry. "I'm so sorry. James has just gone to check on her and see if she is coming back. Perhaps just leave the plate in her place for now."

The waitress deposited the plate of food and went to check on the next door table. The rest of us resumed eating and chatting. A few minutes later, James returned and sat back down taking a huge swig of his lager. It looked like he needed it. He looked frustrated.

"Are you ok, mate?" asked Harry. "Is she coming back?"

"No," replied James. "She's gone home. I've ordered and paid for an Uber for her. In fact, I won't be seeing her again. I've just told her we are over. I'm sick of her behaviour. There is absolutely no fun in her anymore."

"Sorry mate," replied Harry. "But maybe it's for the best."

"For sure," confirmed James. "To be honest I'd been thinking of finishing with her for ages. She's turned into a right moaning whinger and I'm sick of it. I'd much rather be single again. Anyway, let's forget about her. I'm sorry if her behaviour has ruined the evening."

"Not at all, James," piped up Molly. "At least there will be some Prosecco for us now."

Everyone laughed, and the tension at the table eased considerably.

"Right, well, shall we share out her steak?" questioned Harry.

James and Harry split the steak between them and then passed her plate over for Molly and me to divide up her chips. There was no point in letting the amazing food go to waste.

"Well, if everyone is pitching in, I'll have the salad," stated George.

I handed the plate to George and he scraped the plate clean of the remaining salad which was topped with an absolutely sumptuous dressing.

The empty plate got handed back to James and returned to the table, and everyone resumed eating. James kindly topped up our Prosecco glasses and ordered another round of pints for the men. Now that the tension had disappeared, the group chat got louder and there was a lot more laughing. Everyone was at ease and the food was simply delicious. George clearly felt more relaxed now and joined in the chat a lot more. Harry and James made sure to include him in their conversations and everyone seemed to have fun. It's surprising what a difference just one person's behaviour can make to the dynamic of the group.

When it came to paying the bill, James tried to pay for Nat's meal, but everyone agreed that it was fine for us to just split the overall bill by 5 instead of 6. That way it was just a few pounds extra for everyone rather than a lot extra for James. He tried to insist that wasn't fair on everyone else who didn't even know they were tagging along, but he was shot down. He offered to buy the next round of drinks and of course we all agreed to that.

We moved on to a cocktail bar further down the street and James bought the initial round for everyone. We'd all had a fair bit to eat and drink, so the mood was buoyant. James returned from the bar with a tray containing a bottle of Prosecco, three pints and six shots of baby Guinness.

"You can't count, James," I laughed. "There are only five of us now."

"Bugger, you're right," James replied. "I forgot. Never mind. I'm happy to have an extra baby Guinness. They are delicious."

We all clinked the shot glasses together and downed them in one. The delicious smooth and creamy mixture was easy to drink with a great aftertaste. Molly came and sat next to me, while George resumed talking with the boys.

"Well, that wasn't much of a surprise," whispered Molly to me. "I didn't think that James and Nat would last."

"It was slightly awkward, but he doesn't seem at all bothered about having to end their relationship," I replied.

"I think it had finished a few weeks ago really. He just hadn't got around to taking that final step," replied Molly.

"He did mention to me at breakfast recently that things weren't going well. But of course, I've not met her before, so I didn't know how factual that was," I replied.

"She used to be really nice, but she has changed massively over the last few months," said Molly. "Maybe the nice Nat was just a front, and actually she's just insecure and possessive. I don't think bringing her out with you was a good plan – she must know that you and James dated previously, and he still carries a bit of a torch for you."

I glanced at George, but he was engrossed in his conversation with Harry and James.

"Well, I don't know about that, but we've always got on well," I confirmed.

"I think you and James were really good together initially. But of course, the timing has never been right as he wasn't really over Jasmine initially, and then you were with Jack when they split up. You've never been single at the same time since, and of course, now you've met George and you seem to like him a lot," said Molly.

"I do like George. He's a good person and he's great fun to spend time with. But, of course I know he's going away for eight weeks soon, and that's at the back of my mind as well," I replied.

"Eight weeks is nothing. That flies by," replied Molly. "If it's meant to work out, it will."

Harry stood up and walked over to us. He picked up the Prosecco bottle which was still half full.

"Do you need some more Prosecco ladies?" he asked.

"I don't think so," I replied. "I'm going to head home shortly. I think I'm getting to the limits of my drinking without having a raging hangover tomorrow."

"I agree," said Molly. "I've had the optimum amount now. Enough to be merry and have had a good time, but not so much that tomorrow gets written off."

I laughed. I tend not to really suffer much from hangovers, but Molly often does. As we've got older, we seem to have got a little better at knowing when to stop drinking. It appeared like we had drunk a lot, but actually, Nat had polished off most of the Prosecco in the restaurant.

Harry headed off to the bar and stood waiting to get served. George headed off to visit the gents, and James came and sat down next to me. As Molly saw him lean over to talk quietly to me, she discreetly got up and headed to the ladies, leaving us to chat for a few minutes.

"I'm so sorry about that," said James. "I hope that it didn't ruin the evening?"

"There is nothing to be sorry about," I replied.

"I should have finished with her weeks ago really," he confirmed. "I was just delaying the inevitable I guess."

"A typical man," I laughed. "Burying your head in the sand."

"Guilty as charged," said James. "I'm don't like hurting people, so I was trying to let her down gently, but it's impossible. I should have dealt with it previously, but at least it's over now."

"Did she accept it?" I asked curiously.

"Well, she did argue back a little bit. But only half-heartedly really," said James. "I think she knew deep down that we were over too. She clearly wasn't happy, and neither was I."

"Well, maybe it's for the best then," I said.

"What about you?" asked James. "George seems like a nice guy."

"He's lovely," I responded. "He's fun, he's good looking, he's sporty and he really cares about other people."

James looked thoughtful.

"I'm not sure if I should say this Lily. But you know I've always really liked you. We've never managed to get our timing sorted. Aside from the few weeks that we dated previously, we've never both been single at the same time," commented James.

"It's a bit weird now," I admitted. "I like you too, but we've been friends for a long time, so it would be quite strange to move from friendship back into having a romantic relationship. Plus, I do like George, and I'd like to see how things go with him. Maybe our timing is still not right."

"Well, just keep at the back of your mind that I care immensely about you. That I am fully aware I made the wrong choice when we parted previously, and that I would love to get back with you one day," said James. "But I also really appreciate our friendship, and I'm quite happy to just stick with that if that is what you decide."

"Thanks James. I appreciate that," I replied.

I could see that Harry was headed back to the table carrying three pints, and shortly afterwards George rejoined us. The conversation resumed, and the boys started talking about a forthcoming trip they were planning to go hiking in the Lake District. They even extended an invitation to George, but the trip was when he's in Gambia.

We spent the next hour listening to George tell us about his impending activities in Gambia. He explained to everyone about the charity that Riley Construction had set up nearly a decade ago now. He told us about four previous trips he had taken, and some of the building projects he had been involved with, including last year's project building a medical centre. He then disclosed details of this summer's project of building the school. He even suggested that Harry and / or James might be interested in joining him too, but they didn't think they could get enough time off work to make it viable. George is lucky in that being the son of the founder of Riley Construction means that he can take an annual 'working' sabbatical to carry out the building projects in the third world country.

"Perhaps you could come out, Lily?" suggested George.

"Me?" I laughed. "I'm not sure I'd be much help. I know nothing about building."

"Well, there are plenty of other very important jobs. We also need project managers and co-ordinators to distribute the jobs out and get everyone working together. There are plenty of opportunities, even if you could just come out and join us for a week or two," said George.

"Well, that's certainly food for thought," I replied. "I'll have a think about it."

A few minutes later, I realised that I was exhausted, and it was time to head home.

"Are you coming back tonight Molly?" I asked.

"I'll head back to Harry's," replied Molly. "But we will drop you off first if you like."

"I'm quite happy to walk Lily home," replied George. "If you are happy with that?"

"Yes, of course I am," I replied. "It would be nice to walk back with you, as long as you don't mind?"

"Of course not," said George. "The pleasure is all mine."

I stood up, hugged Molly and then both the boys goodbye, and then George and I headed out of the bar. As soon as we got out into the cooler night air, I started to feel a little better. I was pleased when George took my hand in his and we headed towards home. It's about a twenty minute walk which will give me time to sober up a little.

We meandered home. We held hands the whole way, and George continued chatting about the trip to Gambia. He was really excited that I was potentially considering going to join him for a week or two. Of course, I hadn't approached work about time off yet, but is something I planned to ask this week, when I can catch my boss in a good mood. I do have a couple of weeks holiday to take, but it would need to be during the summer holidays, and I usually avoid taking time off then, to cover those with families who are limited when they can go on vacation.

We soon arrived home and I unlocked the door and led the way inside.

"Would you like to stay with me for the night?" I asked. "Just to sleep though, don't expect any action."

"Are you sure?" replied George. "Of course, I'd love to stay with you. But there is no pressure. I'm quite happy to go home if you would prefer."

"No, I would like you to stay," I said. "I wouldn't have asked you if I wasn't sure. I am really tired though. What with skiing this morning and then a night out, I really do need to get some sleep. It's already past one o'clock in the morning."

"Blimey," said George. "I had no idea it was so late. I'd love to just lie down with you in my arms and go to sleep like that."

After what happened with Leo, I was keen to take things slow. I did like George, and he seemed to be an incredibly lovely, compassionate man. But I didn't want to jump straight into a sexual relationship with him. After all, I'd only known him a few days and I wasn't sure how much of a spark there was between us.

"That's a deal then," I confirmed. "Stay, but we will keep it strictly PG for now. In fact, I really am tired, so let's just go to bed now."

I took George's hand and led him into the bedroom. I had a quick root around in my drawers and found a skimpy pair of shorts and a vest top that I changed into, and I brushed my teeth. I told George to take some toothpaste so that he could at least clean his teeth with his finger. I fully intended to kiss him, so it would be nice if he had cleaned his teeth at least a little bit.

A few minutes later George climbed into bed. He opened his arms and scooped me up. He stroked the side of my face and murmured something to me that I didn't catch.

"What did you say?" I asked. "Sorry, I couldn't hear."

"I just said that I really like you Lily. And I'm happy to be here," said George.

"I'm happy you are here too," I replied.

And with that, I lifted up my head, looked straight into his eyes and slowly moved towards his lips. He kissed me on the lips, and I deepened the kiss. We had a really slow, sensual, lazy kiss that was incredibly nice, but didn't quite blow me away.

As we broke away from each other George just said one word to me.

"Wow."

Well, what to do now? I was adamant that I wasn't going to sleep with George. Not after what happened with the last man that I slept with. And I wasn't sure if I really wanted to. I definitely like George but I wasn't sure how much substance there really was to the connection between us.

I tipped my head back up and kissed him again. Another long and enjoyable kiss. But, this time, I turned myself over, he wrapped his arms around me from behind, and I quietly whispered "Good night George."

"Good night," George responded.

I lay for a few minutes feeling contented, wrapped up in George's arms. I listened to his breathing rate reduce and felt my own heart rate gradually drop as I faded into sleep.

Chapter 15

I woke up on Sunday morning as a ray of sunshine streamed through a gap in the curtains right onto my face. I rolled over to find the bed was empty. George had gone. I wondered if he was elsewhere in the flat, or if he had left. It had been the first night that we had spent together, and it had been nice.

I spied his shoes on the floor next to the bed, so it was probably a good assumption that he was still here. I sat up, listening carefully, to see what I could hear. I could hear some movement in the kitchen. The squeak of a cupboard door open and some clinking noises. I would guess that he was making us a brew each.

I lay back on the pillow and relaxed. I had slept well – much better than normal actually. And a quick check of my watch told me that it was gone 7.30 a.m. so I had slept in a little bit too. I heard the creak of the floorboards as George headed back into the bedroom, carrying two mugs. Hopefully he remembered that it was just tea for me.

"Oh, morning Lily. You are awake I see," said George.

"Morning sexy," I responded. "Yes, I just woke up a couple of minutes ago. How are you?"

"I feel great," smiled George. "It looks like a beautiful day, so we should probably get up and cracking. But I thought a cuppa in bed might be good first. I hope that I remembered correctly that you only drink tea? No sugar, with a touch of milk?"

"Yes, spot on," I replied. "Thank you very much."

"It's no problem at all," said George. "I'm making the most of the coffee here, because once I'm in Gambia, we don't have any mains electricity so making a coffee is a bit more complex."

"Wow," I replied. "It's pretty basic then?"

"Yes," confirmed George. "Of course, most of the country does have electricity as standard now, but some of the more remote places still don't. They either have to run an expensive generator or they have to use renewable energy of some type, or they have to light fires.

"We really do take a lot for granted don't we," I commented.

"That's one of the good things about working in Gambia," remarked George. "Every time I visit it reminds me how lucky we are here. Our definition of poor is so different here to third world countries. Our poor people still have some food to eat, most have houses to live in, they still have TVs, radios, often cars, they can afford to buy clothes and they have fresh, running water. The poor people in Gambia literally have nothing apart from some dirty shoes, a basic hut, no fresh water or sanitation services. It's like another world."

"It must be fulfilling to help communities like that," I commented.

"It is," said George. "I meant what I said last night. It would be great if you could come out to Gambia for a week or two, if you have a chance. There would be plenty for you to help out with and I think you would get a lot out of the experience."

"I will look into it," I promised. "When do you actually leave?"

"I leave this Friday morning," replied George.

"Oh, wow. That's not long then," I commented. "Will we get to see each other before you go?"

"Yes," replied George. "I'll make sure we do. I've got tons to do, as you can imagine, but I could meet up Tuesday night if that works for you?"

"Definitely," I responded. "Let me know when and where please."

At that, George said that he had to leave. What with going to Gambia on Friday morning, he had lots to do, including starting to pack. I asked if he had time for breakfast, but he said that he was already running late and wouldn't bother with breakfast. He had to go and catch up with his family for lunch today as he's not going to be around for some time. George's Dad is one of the patrons of the charity, so he's got lots to talk to him about. The charity is heavily sponsored by Riley Construction, in fact they seem to match whatever money is raised by the group with an equivalent amount. They also allow the paid sabbatical for George, as he wouldn't be able to afford to do the trip otherwise.

Shortly after George left, I called Molly and she confirmed that she would be home tonight so we could have a bottle of wine together. About twenty minutes later I had a text from James asking if I fancied a run. I'd been a bit slack this week, and only run once so far, so I agreed to meet with James for a 10km run from the park. Including the distance to and from the park that would equate to about 15km for me, so a decent length run.

A couple of hours later, I'd had a nice easy jog to the park and was loitering near the bridge waiting for James to arrive. He soon turned up looking mighty fine in his running kit. I still had the occasional pang for him, even though we were just friends. After the usual greetings, we set off running through the aptly named Bluebell Woods, although the bluebells were well over by this time of year. I started by quizzing James about Nat.

"Have you heard from Nat since she left the restaurant yesterday?" I asked.

"Yes, I had a message and a call from her this morning," replied James. "I think she had a hangover and was feeling rather rubbish. She apologised for her behaviour last night. She admitted that she drank too much and was being rather unpleasant."

"So, are you going to try and work through things with her?" I asked.

"No," replied James. "We are done. She did ask me if I would give her another chance, but I'm not interested. We've had too many chats where we talk about why she drinks too much, and why she seems to have the need to criticise and be moody. I can't be bothered anymore. I'd rather be on my own than be with someone that behaves like that."

"I know what you mean," I agreed. "Sometimes it's much easier to be single." I sighed.

"Well, George seems like a good guy. And you seem to like him. Are you seriously considering going out to see him in Gambia?" James asked.

"Yes, I am," I confirmed. "I think it would be an exciting trip if I can get some time off work. I don't mind travelling alone and I'm sure he would meet me at the other end."

"Well, make sure that you look after yourself," replied James. "I know you are a strong, independent woman, but Africa can be a daunting place for anyone."

"Have you been to Gambia yourself?" I asked.

"No, but I've been to South Africa, and I've also been to Senegal which is right next to Gambia," replied James. "So I have a little understanding of what it's like. There's a massive divide between those that have and those that have not."

"That's exactly as I understand it," I replied. "There is money, especially from tourism, going into the countries. But it only seems to line the pockets of the government and the rich. The people that actually need the money don't seem to get any share of it. That's why the work that people like George are doing in the country is so valuable – because they are directly helping those that need it the most."

"It's certainly very commendable," said James. "I'd love to be able to have six or eight weeks off work with full pay. I guess that's the benefit of being the CEO's son."

"Not jealous at all then James," I laughed.

"Just a little bit," confirmed James. "Plus, he's dating you, and that makes me very jealous indeed."

"You had your chance," I said.

"Yes, and stupidly blew it," replied James. "I will forever regret that decision."

"Well, we do have a beautiful friendship as a result," I commented.

"Indeed we do, and that does soften the blow somewhat," said James. "I do love spending time with you, even just as friends. Plus you are a pretty decent running buddy of course."

We left Bluebell Wood and were now running along a country lane which was very quiet. As we came up to a corner, I saw there was a wide grass verge with a man placing a box on the edge of a stream that was meandering along. I wondered what he was doing and commented to James. He agreed that it looked odd, and that he thought it was the driver of a car that had sped past us just as we were climbing a stile to leave the wood a couple of minutes ago. He'd clearly been in a hurry, so it was odd that he was now dumping something, probably rubbish. He must be one of those frustrating fly tippers.

The man glanced furtively over his shoulder and spotted us running along. He jumped up, kicked the box into the stream, and ran back to his car. Jumping in quickly, he slammed the door, started up the engine, and drove off, tyres squealing.

"What on earth?" I started.....

James sprinted off, heading towards the stream and where the box had been.

"What are you doing?" I called.

"I think I know what's going on," yelled James. "Hurry! I need your help."

I sped up as quickly as I could and joined James as he had jumped off the bank into the stream. Luckly it was only about waist deep, and I could see that he was fishing the sodden box out of the water.

"Quick, help me get this up," said James.

I leant down from the bank and grabbed the top half of the box as James pushed from underneath. The box was drenched and heavy, but it seemed like something was moving inside. It suddenly dawned on me that the man had dumped a box of either puppies or kittens or something similar into the stream. What an absolute arse. I do not understand how someone could do something like that.

We struggled to get the box onto the bank as it was starting to disintegrate and had clearly been weighted down with something. I tore at the top flaps of the box and pulled off some gaffer tape. As I opened the box, I could see that it did indeed contain puppies. There must have been about 7 of them. The puppies on the top were moving but the ones on the bottom were still and looked lifeless.

"Quick, get them out," said James. "We might be able to save them."

James ripped off his t-shirt, and grabbed one of the puppies that wasn't moving.

"Quick, copy me," he said.

I grabbed hold of another of the puppies and attempted to do what James was doing. He first laid the puppy on its back, put his hand into its jaws to clear its throat, and then breathed into its mouth. I didn't really know what I was doing, but I attempted to do the same. I don't really know if it helped, but James's puppy was soon moving and squealing. He then grabbed my puppy which was still unresponsive. James managed to get that one moving too, and then he grabbed the final unresponsive one from me and tried to coax that one back to life. Sadly, it wasn't meant to be, and the final puppy didn't start breathing again. It was the one that had been right at the bottom of the box, so probably got crushed. The other puppies were all starting to crawl about, making little yowling noises.

Two of them were hardly wet, and they were making the most noise. The next two were moving tentatively but seemed absolutely fine, and the two that James had revived were starting to yowl more.

"What do we do with the dead puppy?" I asked.

"Well, we can take him home and dig him a little grave," said James. "I don't want to leave him here. That seems really sad."

"How are we going to get them home?" I asked. "We've got nothing to carry them with."

"Um, I'm not sure," replied James. "Actually, my car is at the park, so I can jog back and get it if you stay with the puppies. Then we can decide what we are going to do with them."

We agreed that was the best plan of action, so we gathered up the puppies, using the edges of the wet box, just to keep them penned in while I waited. And then James set off running back to the park, a lot more quickly than we were running previously.

While I was waiting, I picked up and cuddled the puppies in turn. I used James's shirt to dry them off as best I could. They all seemed very skinny, especially the one that had died. He was much smaller than the others, so I guessed that he was the runt of the litter, and probably wouldn't have made it anyway. Whilst I was sad that we had lost one, I was very happy that we had managed to save the other six.

They looked like labrador puppies, but were a mix of black, grey and a few brown ones. I assumed they were mongrels, because if they had been labradors they would have been worth a fair bit of money and probably would have been sold rather than dumped.

Thank goodness we had been out running at the time. I tried to think back and remember what I could about the man that had dumped them, and his car. I really had very few details that I could recall. The man was Caucasian, he was about 5'10" tall although it was hard to judge as I'd mainly seen him crouching down. He was certainly not very tall or very short anyway. He was wearing a green hoodie, blue jeans and white trainers. I didn't see his age as he mainly had his back to us. But I'd guess that he was probably 20's or 30's from how he carried himself.

I have no clue what car he drove. A tatty, blue one was about all I could remember. I didn't even notice what make it was. It was a bit of a boy racer car, but I really couldn't recall any more.

James arrived back with his car and opened up the boot. He has an estate car, so there was plenty of room for the puppies and they couldn't escape anywhere. I said I'd sit in the boot with them, so James removed the parcel shelf to make room for me.

"What are we going to do with them?" I asked.

"Well, I assume that you can't really have them as you only have a flat with no outside area," said James. "I could have them overnight, but I think they are going to have to get taken to a vet or a rescue centre tomorrow as there is no-one home all day at my house to look after them in the week."

"That makes sense. Shall we take them back to yours for now then? Are Molly and Harry at home anyway?" I asked.

"They were heading out when I left, but they are due back soon. So we will have plenty of help looking after them," confirmed James.

As James slowly drove home, I did a bit of Googling on my phone. As it was Sunday afternoon, there wasn't much that we could do to get help. It seemed we could make them a milk replacement formula using cow's milk, water, vegetable oil and egg yolks. That would keep them going for a day or so until we could get them to somewhere that had the knowledge and resources to look after them properly.

Once we got back to James's, he headed out to find a large cardboard box. He managed to source one at the local takeaway, and he put some old carpet and an old towel in the bottom of the box. We gently put the puppies into the box, and then set about making the formula for them. We couldn't really separate the egg yolks from the whites, so we just threw it all in there. I felt fairly sure it would keep them alive and probably be better than just cow's milk. James's neighbour had a baby, so he nipped over there to see if they had an old baby's bottle that he could have. They were happy to donate an old one to us, as they clearly wouldn't want it back again. In fact, just as he was leaving, they managed to find two more old bottles that they didn't want any more. So that would help us considerably.

Upon his return, we fed all of the puppies. Aside from the last one that James revived, the others all drank greedily. And once they had finished, they all lay down and fell asleep. It wasn't really a surprise. The least healthy one only drank a little bit, and then was too lethargic to have any more. We hoped that she was just super tired, rather than incredibly poorly. Once all the pups were asleep, we had time to go and dig a little grave to dispose of the dead puppy. We both felt a bit sombre at that, but decided we had to look on the positive side and celebrate the fact that we had saved six lives rather than mourn the loss of one.

By the end of all this excitement, we collapsed on the sofa. I felt absolutely knackered, and actually rather cold now. I hadn't realised how cold I was getting as I'd been so caught up in the moment. James popped into his bedroom and leant me a pair of jogging bottoms, a clean t-shirt and a hoodie. Once I had changed, I felt much better.

"Tea or wine?" asked James.

"Wine I think," I confirmed. "After all the excitement of the afternoon, I felt like we both deserved a nice glass of wine."

As James disappeared into the kitchen, I heard a key in the lock and in walked Molly and Harry. They were extremely surprised to find me in situ and asked what was going on. I explained about finding the puppies, and Molly came over to look in the box.

"Oh, they are so cute," she exclaimed. "I'm so pleased that you were able to save them. Poor little things. They look like labrador puppies."

"That's what I thought initially," I responded. "But on closer examination I think they are a mix of lab and maybe whippet or something like that. It's hard to tell at the moment as they are so small, and clearly a bit malnourished. They can only be a few days old at the most."

"Where did you find them?" Harry asked as he walked into the room.

I filled both Molly and Harry in on the events of the afternoon. They thought we should report the matter to the police and see if they would do anything. I said I would talk to James and see if he had a good description of the car or the man that had dumped them. At that, James walked into the room with a bottle of wine and four glasses. We all sat down on the floor with our backs against the sofa, looking into the box with wistful faces. James poured the wine and dished out the glasses to us.

"Can we keep them?" asked Molly.

"I'd love to," replied James. "But it's not practical or realistic. We all have full-time jobs so no-one would be here to look after them. Hand-reared puppies need feeding every few hours around the clock.

"How do you know all this?" I asked James. "You even knew how to revive the ones that needed it."

I filled Molly and Harry in on James's ability to resuscitate them and admitted that one hadn't survived so we'd buried it in the garden.

"My aunt used to breed puppies," said James. "I used to help her with them when I was little. I remember that I was there when one litter was being born, and sadly the mum died of a haemorrhage, so she hand-reared the nine puppies from that litter. She said that it was incredibly hard work and that they needed around the clock care. She lived right by us at the time, so I was able to go and help out before and after school. Little did I know that the skills she taught me would come in handy later on."

"Well, we would have lost at least three puppies straight away if you hadn't been able to revive them. I think you are a bit of a hero really," I remarked.

"Thanks," said James. "I'm just glad we were able to save them."

We enjoyed the rest of the evening, laughing and chatting between us. It felt like old times, when we used to double date. I could feel that James had migrated a little along the sofa until we were touching shoulders and legs. It felt good and I was tempted to curl up in his arms, but I knew that I should resist.

"Why don't you both stay over here tonight and help with the puppies?" suggested Harry.

"That's fine with me," said Molly. "What do you think Lily?"

"Is there room for me to stay?" I asked.

"Well, James can sleep on the sofa, you can have James's bed, and Molly will be in with me of course," replied Harry. "Are you happy with that James?"

"Yes, that's fine with me mate," said James. "I'm more than happy to do that. I'll need to feed the pups a couple of times during the night in any case, so Lily is more than welcome to my bed."

"Sorted," confirmed Molly. "Shall we open another bottle of wine?"

"Please do," agreed Harry. "There are two more in the fridge, so plenty to go around."

The evening slid by. We looked after the puppies, and once they'd had a good sleep, we each picked one up for a cuddle. They were indeed incredibly cute, if rather sleepy after their adventures. We steadily made our way through the wine, and later ordered some takeaway pizza. No-one could be bothered to cook, plus there was a two-for-one deal so it was a bit of a bargain. For just under twenty-five pounds, we had four large pizzas delivered.

Later that night, Molly and Harry went off to bed. I cleaned my teeth using a spare toothbrush that Molly happened to have, and then I climbed into James's bed. I was shattered. The bed smelt of James's aftershave, and I felt very warm and contented buried under his quilt. Just as I was drifting off to sleep, there was a tap on the door.

"Who is it?" I spoke softly, conscious that I didn't want to wake anyone else.

"It's just me," whispered James. "Can I come in?"

"Of course you can, it's your room," I laughed quietly.

James opened the door and crept in. He sat on the edge of the bed, and I could see his outline as it wasn't quite dark in the room.

"I thought we could share my bed. I promise to be a total gentlemen, and I won't even try to kiss you," asked James.

"OK," I replied. "That sounds nice actually."

I opened up the duvet to allow James to climb in. He lay down on his back and opened his arm so I could snuggle in. He felt familiar and comfortable. He was warm and smelt lovely. It reminded me of the happy times when we had dated before. And then I remember how he had decided to go back to his old girlfriend and how hurt I had been.

I have to admit, I was so tempted to lift up my head and kiss him. But I had promised myself that I wouldn't do that.

I did trust James implicitly, and I knew that he wouldn't try to persuade me otherwise. I also didn't think that would be fair to George.

"Goodnight Lily," he murmured. I could feel him kiss the top of my head.

"Night James, sleep well," I responded. I did lift my head slightly and I kissed his neck. I really, really wanted to kiss him properly, on his mouth, but I resisted the urge, and just enjoyed the feeling of being snuggled up with him. We were both shattered, so in what felt like no time at all, I could feel myself drifting off to sleep for the second time that night.

Just as I drifted off, I think I heard James say, "It's you, Lily. It's always been you." But I was too tired to focus on it.

Chapter 16

By the time that I woke the next morning, the sun was streaming through the windows. The bed next to me was bare, but the sheets were crumpled. So, I hadn't dreamt that I had shared the bed with James then.

It made me smile just thinking about being cuddled up in his arms. And I had really wanted to kiss him. I was so confused. It had been a long time since I thought that James and I could revitalise what we had previously, and in the meantime, I had developed feelings for George. It's typical really. As soon as you start to feel happy, another man comes along to confuse things.

I climbed out of bed and grabbed James's dressing gown from the back of his door. I then padded out to the kitchen to find James diligently feeding one of the puppies.

"Don't be shy," said James. "Help yourself to a puppy. They all need feeding."

"No problem," I responded. "Shall I make us a drink first though?"

"Yes please," replied James. "Coffee for me. White, no sugar."

I filled the kettle up and set it to boil, and then hunted down the teabags, the coffee, some mugs and milk. A few minutes later we had a hot drink each, and I reached for a puppy and a baby bottle of milk. Most of the puppies were already pretty good at latching on and drinking from the bottle. However, I had picked up the smallest puppy which hadn't yet drunk very much.

"Here," said James passing me a knife. "Make the hole at the end of the baby bottle bigger and then the pup should be able to drink easier."

"That's a good idea," I agreed. I took my time cutting off the end of the teat ensuring that I did it correctly. If it was too big it wouldn't work properly either. When I tried again with the puppy, I could see that this time it was easily consuming the milk. In no time at all, the puppy had finished nearly half the bottle, so I decided that was enough for the moment.

Whilst we steadily worked with the remaining puppies, James told me that he'd spoken to a rescue centre the other side of Castledyke, and that we could take them over there at twelve noon today. They would happily take over the responsibility of raising them and would look to rehome them when they were a little older. I felt sad that they would be leaving us, but glad that they would be well looked after and get the chance of a forever home with a family.

Later that day we dropped the puppies off at the rescue centre, and helped them get settled in. James and I then headed to the police station and gave a statement about how we found them and where they were now. I was a bit disappointed that the police weren't really interested but neither of us were able to remember any distinguishing features of the man in question or his vehicle. They did say that they would attempt to locate some CCTV footage, but that we weren't to get our hopes up.

After all the excitement of the last 24 hours, it was definitely time to chill out and rest up before work tomorrow. I also had to figure out if it would be a good thing to go and visit George in Gambia. Or, would that be the wrong thing to do, especially as I had been rather enjoying the time spent with James. What to do? I'm a great believer in grabbing opportunities with both hands, so was interested in going to Gambia. But it was very early days with George, and I definitely felt a little torn with interest from James too. I concluded that I needed a nice chill out night with Molly.

A few hours later, Molly and I were tucked up on the couch at our home. It wasn't often that Molly stayed at home now, but she appreciated that I needed a bit of one-on-one time with her. We had a bottle of wine open in front of us, and I had poured us both a glass.

"So what's the latest with you then Molly?" I asked.

"Well, Harry and I are obviously looking to move in together as you know. But we have been discussing the merits of buying somewhere together rather than renting," Molly replied.

"Wow, that's a big commitment," I exclaimed. "That's really serious."

"Yes, I know," replied Molly. "But we are serious. We've talked about getting married in due course, although neither of us are that fussed about a piece of paper at this stage. We have discussed having children in a year or two, so we feel like we need to be thinking long-term rather than throwing money away on renting."

"That's fantastic news Molly. I'm so excited for you." I grinned like an idiotic Cheshire cat.

"Thanks, Lily. I'm really excited too. It feels fantastic that I think I've finally found 'the one'," said Molly. "But what about you? How's things going with George? And did something happen with James this weekend? I did happen to notice that he had disappeared off the couch last night."

"I'm really confused to be honest," I admitted. "Things seem to be going really well with George. He is such a great guy. The thing with James this weekend has come a little out of the blue really. I know we've always got on great, but our timing has always been off. And it was only this weekend that I have seriously considered getting back with James. He really hurt me last time, so it's a big step to make."

"It's typical that you've met George at the same time as James has just split up with his girlfriend. And now of course, George is going away for a couple of months. How do you feel about that?" asked Molly.

"Well, it's not ideal timing. I've only known him less than two weeks. But he does seem like a truly good person. And I do fancy him. But at this point, eight weeks seems like a really long time, although I know that in the grand scheme of things it's a drop in the ocean really," I said.

"And how do you feel about going to see him in Gambia? Like he asked," replied Molly.

"Well, as you know, I love to grab hold of opportunities that open up to me. But it's also quite a big deal as I've known him such a short time. And the part of Gambia that I would be going to is hardly a tourist area. It's very remote, and I'd be virtually camping out with George in the middle of nowhere. It's quite a risk for a single lady. I'd be placing a lot of trust in George to keep me safe, and of course, he will be busy working on the school project. I'd love to help, but I'm hardly equipped with the best DIY skills."

"It is a bit of a dilemma," agreed Molly. "If you'd been seeing him for a few months, it would be a different story, but you've literally just met him. What do you think you are going to do?"

"I really don't know. I had pretty much decided that I would go, if I could get the time off work. But then after this weekend with James, I'm a little undecided," I replied.

"How are you feeling about James?" asked Molly. "Did anything happen between you?"

"No, we just shared his bed and had a cuddle. I didn't even kiss him although I really wanted to at the time," I said. "It's really confusing as it's been such a quick about turn. Because he had a girlfriend, I hadn't seriously considered him as an option. But now I think it might be different. In fact, just as I was drifting off to sleep, he said something slightly strange."

"What did he say?" asked Molly.

"It's you, Lily. It's always been you," I replied. "Well, at least, I think that's what he said. I was drifting off to sleep at that point so I can't be completely sure."

"I did happen to overhear him talking to Harry about you," said Molly.

"Oh, really? What did he say?" I asked.

"He said that he had no idea why it had taken him so long to finish with Nat. He hadn't been happy with her for a long time, but he just finds it hard to hurt people. And he knew she wouldn't take it well. But he said that he's wanted to be with you ever since you were together before - prior to Jack. He told Harry that he only dated Nat because you were with Jack."

"Oh, wow," I commented. "He really does like me then. His timing is bad though. Why did he have to wait until another man had come into my life? Talk about making things hard for yourself."

"Well, that's often the way isn't it. I guess he was giving you time to get over things going so wrong with Jack, and then got a bit side-tracked with Nat. Typical bloke – letting things go on long after they should have done. Men are so good at burying their head in the sand rather than being decisive. I think he was hoping that Nat would finish with him so that he didn't have to do it. I guess he didn't know that you were going to meet George while he was messing about."

"What a screw-up. Well, I just need to figure out what I'm going to do," I replied.

Molly picked up the empty wine bottle and asked if I wanted a top-up. I said no, and that I was going to head off for bed. It had been a busy weekend and I was tired. I was no closer to deciding what I was going to do, but hopefully a good night's sleep might make things clearer.

Chapter 17

I had arranged to meet George for coffee on Tuesday evening. As he was leaving for Gambia later in the week, he was super busy with things to do, so he only really had time to meet with me for an hour or so. I still hadn't decided if I was going to fly to Gambia to meet up with him. It was a really difficult decision to make as I had known him such a short time. Plus, it seemed like there was a good chance of getting together with James again if that was what I decided. So, I was quite happy that it was just an hour for coffee as it could be a little awkward between us if I decided not to go and see him.

When I arrived at the coffee shop, George was already there and had purchased me a tea and a chocolate brownie. Considering how short a time I had known him he was getting to grips with my likes and dislikes. George stood up, gave me a kiss on the cheek and a hug, and pulled out my chair for me. He is such a gentleman, and that is one of the things that attracted me to him.

I was feeling rather nervous as I wasn't sure what I was going to say to George. After a couple of pleasantries, we started talking about the trip.

"Are you excited to get out there and get working on the school?" I asked.

"I can't wait to get going. There are six of us flying out together and we will be joining up with a couple of people that live in the area and then about a dozen of the locals. The complete group is around 20 and we hope that the school will be finished in 12 weeks. I'm planning to be there for eight weeks which I feel is when I can be most productive. Once the structural work is done, there isn't a requirement for so many people to be there," explained George.

"It does sound like a challenge," I commented.

"It is indeed, especially due to the lack of basic services out there. We setup a camp where we need to be effectively self-sufficient other than buying in some food. Riley Construction send over a convoy of lorries with materials, portaloos, and the essential tools and food that we need. Other than that, it's up to us," said George.

"Is it safe?" I asked.

"Well, it's in a very rural area, so there is not much interest in us really. As it's off the beaten track, it's probably as safe as anywhere in Gambia," replied George. "Are you thinking about coming to see me?"

"I'm definitely thinking about it," I replied. "I'm usually up for a challenge but I do have a few things that I'm a little concerned about."

"Go on," said George.

"Well initially, I know that you've got a lot of work to do in a very short time, and I don't want to impact on that priority. I know that you are going to be very busy, and I don't want to get in the way," I explained. "Then, I am a little concerned about the security side of things. Travelling to you from the airport may not be straightforward, and it's not like I would be able to stay in a nearby hotel. Lastly, and please don't take offence at this, but I don't really know you. We literally only met just over a week ago, so it seems really quick to be going abroad to be with you," I said.

"No offence taken Lily," replied George. "And they are all legitimate concerns. We do have a lot of work to do, and I'm not expecting you to pitch in with structural work of course. But there is also a lot of managing people, feeding people, moving materials and tools around, and ensuring that everyone is where they need to be and focussing on the main priorities. That's all work that can be done without prior experience, just a good bit of common sense and co-ordination skills. With regards to security, we do have a couple of local guys that work throughout the night to guard the materials and construction site, so it's not quite as bad as it sounds. And, I promise to behave like a gentleman at all times. Lastly, we would ensure that one of our drivers picks you up from the airport and brings you straight to the site, so you wouldn't have to worry about that. Of course, I'd like to do that myself but it's a four hour round trip and my time is probably better spent on site."

"Do I need to decide now?" I asked.

"Of course not," replied George. "I'm there for a minimum of eight weeks, and we can chat on the phone when it's possible. I don't really know what the communications are like – Facetime will probably be difficult but it's usually possible to get some signal for messages and even for audio calls. We also hope to have some access to Starlink, the internet provided by Elon Musk, so that's an option. We've been told that there is limited satellite coverage by Starlink in Gambia now, although it's only recently been introduced so we haven't yet been able to test it. But that might make all the difference."

"Well, that sounds like a great opportunity for the economy of the country. Surely having reliable internet opens up many opportunities for a developing country," I commented.

"Yes exactly," agreed George. "The internet nowadays is really a necessity for economic growth. You can decide at any point if you want to come out and join me. You could come for a week or two and you could bring a friend. I can arrange the transfer from the airport with no issues, and then you'd just be bedding down with us in large tents."

"It sounds exciting," I replied. "I haven't yet heard back from work about time off, but I will do soon. And the idea of bringing a friend is interesting as well. Although it's not really Molly's cup of tea. She hates camping. I think she would be horrified."

"It's not for everyone," laughed George. "If she doesn't like camping, she probably wouldn't appreciate the trip to be honest."

"But I'm sure one of my other friends might be up for an adventure. Let me look into that and get back to you," I suggested.

"That sounds ideal," responded George. "As I said, there is no hurry to decide, and no pressure. I won't take offence if you don't come. And I will look forward to seeing you on my return. But if you can come, I'd love it, and I think you would too."

We continued chatting whilst finishing our drinks. The chocolate brownie was absolutely delicious. I don't really have a sweet tooth, but I am partial to a bit of brownie. And it was really nice to chat to George some more. He has a really easy way about him. There is no pressure. He's just great fun, easy-going, honest and seems totally trustworthy. I really do enjoy his company which considering how short a time I've known him is quite impressive.

Twenty minutes later George really had to go. He said that he had a list of things to get completed before he leaves for Gambia, and time was running out. I probably wouldn't get to see him again for a while, so as he left he took me in his arms for a massive hug. And gave me a wonderfully warming kiss which made me sad that he was leaving. Whatever happened, it would be a while before I saw him again, and even though I'd only known him such a short time, I was sad to see him go.

The rest of the week passed quickly, and I knew that George had left for his trip. We had swapped numbers now, so I had the option to WhatsApp him, but of course, we didn't have any idea what the connectivity in Gambia would be like, so it might only be possible intermittently. Still, he had been quite communicative up until the point that he left.

On Friday morning I had a message from James to see if I wanted to meet up with him. As it happened, I had promised to go to the cinema with mum as there is a film that she really wanted to see. So, I told him I'd see him at parkrun and maybe we could go for breakfast afterwards. I hadn't seen much of my mum recently, so I didn't want to let her down. As it turned out, we had a great evening. We watched her choice of film, which was actually brilliant, and then we had a meal out afterwards, just the two of us. It was something that we only do occasionally, so I really appreciated spending the time with her.

Saturday, otherwise known as parkrun day, was a beautiful summer's day. I jogged quietly to the park in good time to fulfil a quest for information. There were quite a few people wearing Castledyke Runners tops, so I had a chat to one of them and found out who the overall organiser was. She happened to be there today, so I spoke with her about joining the club. She was very welcoming and told me that they had over 100 members in total, although probably only 50 of them ran regularly on club nights.

Just before the briefing I saw James jog into the park. I felt my heart rate rise and I couldn't help but beam out a smile which was instantly reciprocated when he spotted me. And then I felt that familiar feeling of butterflies in my stomach. I'd had that rather delicious feeling the last couple of times I had met up with James, and it felt pretty good. For a long time, I had only considered a friendship with James, but things seemed to be hotting up between us. Certainly my body was responding to him, even if my brain wasn't.

James jogged over and gave me a rather nice hug, albeit a little sweaty. He did smell divine though which certainly helped, and I hoped that he felt the same. He picked me up and swung me around like he hadn't seen me for ages, and then seemed rather embarrassed that he had done that without thinking.

"Sorry Lily," he said. "I don't know what came over me then. I just had this sudden urge to pick you up." James had gone red and looked at the floor.

"It's fine James," I replied. "Don't worry. It's good to see you too."

James looked straight at me and his eyes twinkled. Gosh, he is hot.

At that, it was time for the briefing, so we both stayed quiet as directed. We listened to the usual instructions and then had a few rounds of applause for the volunteers and a couple of milestones. And then we were ready for the off.

James asked me if I wanted to run together, but I told him to just do his own thing and I'd catch up with him at the end. At that came the inevitable 3, 2, 1… parkrun…….

And we were off. There was the usual stampede at the beginning and I was swept along, running much more quickly than I felt comfortable. But things soon settled down, and about three or four minutes in I was able to ease off the pace a little without too many people passing me. I do find it a little demoralising if lots of people pass me, but equally I don't want to get stuck behind lots of slow people either.

I felt pretty good today. Usually by the time you are about ten minutes in, you will have a good idea if you are going to achieve a good time. I hadn't actually been running much in the last week, so my intention was to run as best I could but also try to enjoy it. Whilst I do enjoy attempting to run a PB, if you try that every week it becomes rather daunting. And it was pretty warm today, so I was glad that I had brought along some water for the end.

By the time I had got to the last lap, I was regretting not bringing my running bottle (where you put your hand through the middle of it so it's not actually annoying to run with). It was truly hot, I was sweating buckets and really needed a drink. My Garmin was telling me that I had been running at a good consistent pace, but it seemed a long way to the finish where my water would be available to me. Five minutes later I crossed the finish line in a time of roughly twenty-six minutes (according to my watch). I was happy with that as I didn't feel that I was running flat out, yet I certainly wasn't hanging around either. It was a good solid effort, especially considering the temperatures. I immediately made my way to my water bottle and chugged at least half of it down.

I could see that James had already been scanned and already looked cool, calm and collected. I headed over to the scanning line and waited until it was my turn. I presented my barcode and finish token, and once scanned it got popped into a bucket ready for the token sorting process.

After chatting to a couple of other people, James and I met up and walked towards the café which we frequented for breakfast, along with a number of other tables full of parkrunners. I think one of the busiest times for the café is post-parkrun.

We ordered what we wanted – I had Eggs Benedict and James had a Full English.

"So how was your run today?" asked James.

"It was good actually – not a world-beating time, but definitely was a strong effort today," I replied. "How about yourself?"

"I had a good solid run today – I finished in just under 21 minutes" replied James.

"Oh my, that is speedy," I commented.

"So, what's going on with you since I saw you last," asked James. "Has George gone to The Gambia now?"

I brought James up to speed with everything, including telling him that George had suggested I travel with a friend if I wanted to go and join him for a week or two in Gambia.

"And do you want to go and see him?" asked James. "Are you and him dating now?"

"No, definitely not," I told him. "I do enjoy spending time with him, but we are not a couple in any way. I've really only met him a handful of times, and he's going away for quite a while, so I wasn't jumping into anything. Anyway, there are other complications too."

"And what might the other complications be?" asked James.

At that I looked at James, then promptly looked at the table while feeling myself turn bright red with embarrassment.

"Oh, I see," said James. "Well, I think I do. Do I detect that you might have some feelings developing for someone else perhaps?"

"Um, um, well, maybe," I stammered.

James took my hand and looked into my eyes with that searching, beautiful gaze of his. "Well, I think that person is a very lucky man indeed."

"It's complicated," I explained. "You really hurt me the first time when we dated, and we then got back to a really nice friendship. I don't want to do anything to jeopardise that because I love you being part of my life, but I can't deny that I am starting to develop feelings for you over and above friendship."

"And what about George?" asked James quietly. "Do you have feelings for him?"

"I like him, and I enjoy his company. But I'm not sure that the chemistry element is quite there," I replied.

"Well, how about I come to Gambia with you? After all, it's not like Molly would fancy it," said James.

Well, that blew me away. I hadn't considered taking James or any other man in fact. I had really only thought about asking Molly but had already admitted to myself that it's not really her sort of thing. She won't go camping in this country, let alone abroad. And when George suggested I bring a friend along, I don't think he meant a man either.

"Um, it's a thought," I mumbled.

"Well, I think it's a great idea. I've got a couple of weeks leave that I need to take, I'd be a massive asset to the team with my engineering background and I'm not afraid of a bit of hard labour," said James.

The more he talked, the more it did actually make sense. Other than the obvious elephant in the room – that George was inviting me over because he fancies me and didn't intend for me to turn up with another guy that is also interested in me. But, James would be an asset to the team, rather than a potential liability like me.

We continued to chat for quite some time on the topic. It turned out that James had done some volunteering for a similar group in Ethiopia a few years before, so he really was well equipped to join the team. It would really depend on what George thought about the situation. He might jump at the chance to have James join the team, despite the potential personal conflict. Equally, he might not be interested in having him at all.

James and I agreed that I would suggest the option to George and see what his thoughts were. I always try to be open and honest, and, as a single woman, it's not like anyone has any claim on me. I literally have had a couple of dates with George, and an ongoing friendship with James, that could possibly develop into more. Of course, there is history with James, but everyone would be aware of the situation.

Later that evening I messaged George, asking him to give me a call if he was able to. Early evening on Sunday, I received a call from him, and the reception wasn't bad.

I explained the situation. That James wanted to offer his services and accompany me to Gambia. There was a silence at the other end and then George asked why he wanted to come. I explained about James's engineering background, and the previous volunteer experience he had in Ethiopia a few years back, and George started to get excited.

"It sounds like he'd be an ideal candidate to join the team," George said. "And we could really do with some more engineering expertise to be honest. Plus, he's clearly not afraid of hard work. It would be ideal for him to join the project."

"Well, that sounds like a good plan then. It would reassure me about the security side of things and would mean that I wouldn't need to travel alone," I agreed.

"Can I ask one question though please?" said George. "What's the situation between you and James? I know you used to date a couple of years back, but is there anything going on now?"

"Look, I'd rather be completely open and honest with you," I said. "James and I are just good friends. Yes, we did date some time ago but only for about six weeks, and then he rekindled a relationship that he had been in previously. Ever since then we have just been friends. And, whilst I do like him, it's not progressed beyond that."

"The way I see things is this," said George. "You and I have literally had a couple of dates and enjoyed each other's company. But it's not progressed further than a few kisses and cuddles. You and James have history, but the current status is also just friends. So, coming on this trip will give you a chance to get to know both of us a little more. I'm a realist, and I'm a great believer in fate. If you and I are meant to be, then we will work out regardless of James coming or not. If James comes, there is a chance that you may decide you have more feelings or more in common with him, but if that's the case, then it's better that you find out now rather than later."

"Wow," I exclaimed. "That's a very mature way to look at it."

"Well, we could desperately do with James's expertise on the project, so that is swaying me slightly. But, as long as we are all open and honest and respectful with each other, I can't see why we can't all be in Gambia, work together and spend time together, and just see where things end up. What do you think?" George asked.

"I think that sounds like a good plan. And I'm happy to go with it," I confirmed.

We spent a few more minutes on the phone chatting about dates, logistics and George asked if I could please bring some Nutella with me. You really couldn't make it up. I said I'd sort out dates and travel arrangements with James, and let George know. He would send the camp's driver to pick us up once we had flown out. He also told us that we needed to get to the doctors asap as we would need some vaccinations, especially Yellow Fever, Hepatitis A and possibly Tetanus.

James and I both were in to see the doctors the very next day, and we got our vaccinations sorted. We were also prescribed malaria tablets. We also checked that our passports were up to date, and I got clearance from work for the required time off.

Two weeks later, I was frantically packing. It was hard to know what to take, but George had told me to just take casual, working clothes as we would be based at camp the whole time. Last weekend, James had told me more about his experiences working in Ethiopia, so I had some idea what to expect. Aside from that Saturday afternoon catch up over coffee, I hadn't seen James much as he had been away working during the week. I'd refrained from going out, as the plane tickets were not cheap, and my savings were a little sparse.

The next morning, at 3am, I was waiting outside for James to pick me up. He'd booked his car into the airport parking, so at least I didn't have to worry about that. I shivered as even though it was summer, the air was still cold at that time of night. As I waited, I thought about the trip to come. I was looking forward to seeing George again, and also looking forward to spending some time with James.

As I saw a car approach, headlights flashed. This was it. The adventure was about to begin.

Chapter 18

A few hours later, James and I were sitting in the Wetherspoons café at the airport. James whipped out his phone and ordered online for us. Within just a few minutes, our food and drinks had arrived. We both had a Full English breakfast with a glass of Prosecco and orange juice. It seems like a tradition to have just a small glass of something to celebrate the start of a holiday – even if it will be a working holiday. A tradition that James and I appeared to share.

The journey to the airport was a couple of hours long, and we had chatted enthusiastically. James had confessed that he was really happy to be travelling with me. He reiterated that he regretted splitting up with me previously, but that he was happy to stay good friends if that was what I decided. He also did reassure me that he would like to be more than friends but was happy to wait and see what happened. James also told me that he was excited to be going to Gambia and being part of the school building project. He was looking forward to meeting the locals, especially the children, and working with the rest of the team.

I have to admit, I had been thinking a lot about James recently. It was quite natural to have had some walls up to protect myself, especially considering that James had hurt me before, but I couldn't quite stop my thoughts from turning to him regularly. Of course, it doesn't help that he is extremely good looking, enjoys similar adventures to me, and we get on so well. And the chemistry that was between us originally was still there, but I had chosen to ignore it for quite some time. It's amazing what the power of thought can do.

It was time to board our plane. As we walked to the gates, it was incredibly busy, so James took hold of my hand. It felt really good, and I felt happy, secure and protected.

Later that day we touched down in Banjul International Airport. The flight had taken around six hours, and I'd managed to sleep for about three hours. I also managed to watch a movie and chat to James. James had clearly been doing some research on Gambia as he was quite knowledgeable about the country. Apparently, it's called The Gambia rather than just Gambia because it was named by the Portuguese who named it after 'The River Gambia' therefore it became known as 'The Gambia'. It also used to be more closely tied to its neighbouring country Senegal, and was actually referred to as Senegambia for a very long time.

Gambia is the smallest country in Africa. It's only about thirty miles long and is bordered on both sides by Senegal. It follows a river and is actually smaller than Yorkshire. Gambia used to be quite central to the slave trade and was used as a waypoint for the collection of slaves. I got off the plane feeling rather more educated and quite fresh - but that didn't last long.

Once we picked up our luggage, we made our way towards the exit. We were being collected by a man called Lamin, but unfortunately, we couldn't find him. We decided that I would wait at the designated meeting point and James would go and find us some caffeine as we were both starting to flag a little. Whilst James was gone, a man approached me. I'd seen him loitering nearby and he had kept flicking glances at me. I had initially thought that it might have been Lamin, but clearly it wasn't as he didn't approach until I was alone.

"You come with me. I am your transport," he said and gesticulated to me in broken English.

"Are you from Riley Construction?" I asked.

"Yes, yes. They send me," he replied. I was not convinced. George had told me that Lamin was tall, extremely friendly and with a beaming smile. This man had none of these features.

"What is my name?" I asked.

"You come with me," he repeated.

"I need to wait for my friend. He's gone to get coffee," I replied.

"No, he's left. You need to come with me," he reiterated.

"I don't think so. I don't think you are here to pick me up at all. You don't even know my name. Where would you take me?" I asked.

"I take you to your hotel," replied the man.

At that point I was absolutely sure that this man was not Lamin, so it was time to act.

"If you don't leave me alone, I'm calling security right now," I responded firmly.

At that, the man scurried off across the airport, and soon faded into the crowds. That was a close call. Who knows where I might have ended up if I had believed him. Luckily, I'm not quite that gullible.

A few minutes later James had returned with drinks. I explained what had happened and he was incredibly concerned. He put his arm around me and promised that he wouldn't leave me alone again. That did put my mind at ease, and I relaxed a little.

Twenty minutes later, a man exactly meeting Lamin's description rushed up to us. He was holding a sign saying 'Welcome Lily and James.' There was no doubt that this was indeed Lamin. He apologised effusively for being late and said that the traffic was diabolical. It was time to leave the airport and see a little of the country.

As we headed out towards the vehicle park, the wall of heat hit us. I love that feeling that you get when you leave an air-conditioned building and go into a hot country. It's blissful. Lamin steered us towards a Jeep, and we slung our belongings in the back and climbed in. Lamin had perfect English and gave us a bit of a running commentary on the area. The first thing I noticed as we left Banjul was the sheer amount of rubbish dumped. There were piles of plastic, metal, railings and just absolute crap all over the place. There were also lots of mangy looking dogs and cats hanging around.

The roads had gradually turned into dirt tracks as we left the urban area behind. It was now clear why we were travelling in a Jeep. The school building project was taking part in a very remote area near the border of Senegal. When I asked what the conditions and facilities were like, Lamin explained that there were limited services, sometimes running water, and no electricity just yet. Of course, we had generators in camp, so had the power that we needed, and plans were afoot to get electricity to the area in due course.

The nearest main settlement, a cross between a town and a village was around ten miles from camp. The locals involved in the project generally shared vehicles to get to the school. The school was part of a small community of buildings that were being built. The medical centre had already been built, and was staffed, and there were a handful of locals that had moved to the area. Some of them lived in small huts with corrugated iron roofs. There were some open sewers around and limited clean water. But, the local services were in the process of being upgraded. A lot more investment had been promised by the government and by various other parties to develop the area. Riley Construction owned some Starlink internet kit so there was some connectivity to the internet in camp. It was a little variable but did work to some extent.

I was quite glad that James had come with me. I was a little shaken up by the man that had approached me at the airport. I told Lamin what had happened, and he shook his head sadly. He explained that it's a very common occurrence, and single ladies especially will be targeted. I asked where I might have ended up, and he explained that the locals are just desperate for money, and I more than likely would have been ok as long as I had some funds to pay them off. It wasn't often that tourists got killed, but muggings and being conned or blackmailed were a common occurrence.

As we approached a town, the children came out to see who was passing by. They came running out to the Jeep until we had a swarm of around thirty children following behind us. The lack of road meant that it was difficult to outdrive them, so we just had to watch them holding out their hands and begging. Lamin explained that they wanted sweets, money and food. He told us it was best not to give them anything or they behaved even worse. Eventually, after a mile or so they gave up, and headed back towards home.

Around forty minutes later, Lamin informed us that we were approaching the camp. I was very excited, especially when I saw some monkeys in the trees. I hadn't spotted any up until this point, but when I looked closely, I could see that there were quite a few evident. Most were quiet but some smaller monkeys were playing together jumping on and off the tree trunks. It was so cute. I'd not seen monkeys in the wild before, other than at a wildlife or safari park. When I pointed them out to Lamin, he told me that they were vervet monkeys, one of several types of monkeys found natively in Gambia.

We shortly pulled up and parked next to three larger vehicles, all carrying various bits of equipment and materials. There was a local man, apparently called John, although I'm guessing this isn't his real name, leaning against one of the vehicles. It seems that they always have to leave someone guarding the vehicles twenty-four hours a day, otherwise things disappear.

"Don't you find it frustrating that the locals will steal things?" I asked Lamin.

"Yes, of course we do. But you also must understand that some of the people are desperate and genuinely have no money. The Gambia is one of the poorest countries in the world despite extensive tourism. When the tourists arrive, they are told by the travel representatives that it's dangerous to leave their hotel. As a result, they stay within the hotel complex, and any money they spend ends up being pocketed by the often foreign-owned hotel chains. None of the money filters down to the local people," Lamin explained.

"That's so sad. Are there not shops, restaurants and such like that tourists could go to?" I asked.

"There is," replied Lamin. "But because the majority of them don't leave the hotels, they never get to find them. It's very hard for the locals to earn a living. And the locals are generally very friendly. Yes, they will barter for trade, and they may try and overcharge you. But just be firm and friendly with them and you get on fine. The tourists are generally safe, despite what the travel operators tell them."

"That is such a shame," agreed James. He's been quiet on the journey. Just soaking up the scenery and listening to my chattering with Lamin. "Hopefully we will get some time to go out of the camp while we are here."

"I'm sure we will be able to get a couple of days out," I replied. "We have chosen to come here ourselves."

Lamin explained that it would be fine to take a day or two out for exploring, but that it would be best to get a local guide. They would be able to take good care of us, and provide a vehicle for us to get around in.

As we disembarked from the Jeep, I heard my name being called. It was George. He came walking quickly over to us and enveloped me in a hug.

"It's great to see you Lily, I'm so happy you have arrived," said George. "You too James mate, your coming on board the project is fabulous. We are so grateful to have your expertise."

"It's a pleasure George," replied James. "I'm truly glad to be here. And I know Lily was a little wary of travelling alone, so I was glad to keep her company."

"Great to see you George," I said. "You're looking really well."

George was indeed looking good. He was looking much more tanned than when I saw him last, as well as much leaner.

George detached himself from me and gave James a manly handshake. He then suggested he showed us around the camp. Where we were currently standing were a handful of vehicles of varying sizes, and some piles of building materials that were clearly ready to be used. As we walked, I could see that there were a couple of portacabins and a series of portaloos. In the distance, I could see what looked like a number of Army tents. There were also a number of gazebos and probably 20 people loitering around.

"Has worked stopped for the day?" I asked.

"Yes," replied George. "It's nearly seven pm and we are done for the day. We are just sorting out food for everyone, then we will sit around a campfire and chill out. One guy has a guitar and sometimes he gets everyone singing. It's fun."

"How safe is it?" I asked. "Am I good to wander around camp on my own?"

"Yes, absolutely," said George. "You are perfectly safe here. During the evening and throughout the night, we have patrols around the camp to ensure that nothing is stolen and everyone is safe. Well, it's more to stop the materials and equipment being nicked really. We've never had any issues with people being hurt here. The locals appreciate that we are trying to help and so generally are very friendly."

I felt much happier at this. It's hard to know what to expect really. I've never been to a developing country before. It's certainly not what I was expecting. The surprising part is the contrast between the beauty of the scenery and the country, and the piles of rubbish and open sewers around, and the huge difference between the beautiful hotels and the really rough conditions that the locals live in.

George told us that last year there were no services at all. Things are definitely improving, and the water supply is being addressed, as is electricity to the region. Of course, camp is more or less self sufficient, but the community will only be able to expand as services become available.

In the less remote areas, the services are significantly better, but the area where the build is taking place is particularly remote, so it's a little like looking back in time.

However, the camp looks pretty decent, so I think we'll be fine for the next couple of weeks.

We spent the next half an hour being introduced to the other project workers – there were maybe a dozen from the UK who are here for varying durations, anything from two weeks up to a couple of months. Then there are another ten or so locals who are part of the building and security teams. I'm also introduced to one older local lady who seems to be called 'Nan' by most people. It seems her key priority is keeping everyone fed and looked after.

All those involved in the project sleep in the Army tents. I was quite relieved when George told me that they had a spare two-person tent which they had reserved for me, just to give me a little privacy, as I am the only woman staying here. I wouldn't have minded sharing with everyone else, but it's nice to have a little privacy just to change and sleep. There are mosquito nets everywhere, which is something new for me. Whilst we get a handful of mosquitoes back home in the UK, there are loads of them here. Every time you enter a tent you have a second mosquito net inside to prevent the dastardly insects from getting to you during the night. I had been pre-warned to bring lots of insect repellent, so was hopeful that would do its job during the day.

I was pleased to see that both George and James were sleeping closest to my tent, so they weren't very far from me. They had both been allocated cot beds in the army tent which were more like sturdy sun loungers than beds. But offered a little more protection than being directly on the floor. Of course, George had been here for a while already, so he was well settled in and used to their routine.

George suggested that I took ten minutes to get myself changed, freshened up and sorted. Then I should join the others for dinner and a seat around the campfire. The others were already starting to eat and gather around, so I quickly got sorted and then went over to have a chat to Nan. It seems she has a Gambian name that is rather difficult to pronounce. And because she has several grandchildren, everyone just calls her Nan. She seems absolutely lovely, really jovial and uplifting. She told me a little about her family and how much she enjoys looking after the men on camp. She says they really are no different to the boys in her family, getting themselves into trouble and strife. It's obvious from her voice how fond of the team she has become.

Nan then tells me to tuck in before all the men come back for more, leaving me hungry. So, I grab myself a plate and help myself to some of the rather delicious looking food. It's been hours since I've eaten, so I'm starving. There seems to be a mixture to choose from – what looks like chicken, some rice, some potatoes and some vegetables on skewers. I take a small selection of each and head over to the fire to find somewhere to sit. There are a number of chairs kicking around, and some beanbags on groundsheets that have been placed on the floor. As I head over, I see that James is already there, picking at the food on his plate whilst talking to George and a couple of other guys.

I find myself a beanbag and pull it over to join the small group. I gratefully sink down with the plate on my lap and pick up my fork. I am loosely listening to the group chatting about the project. It seems that the foundations are all in and the walls are now being built. The walls are primarily constructed of mud bricks which are made locally. The cement used to bind everything is imported. The roofs are made of wood frames and then are primarily covered with corrugated sheets. Some of the roofs will have solar panels installed on them which will help to produce electricity reducing the reliance on services. There will also be a few grass huts built as additional classrooms. These will hopefully only be temporary but are the quickest way to get the school up and running. There are hundreds of children in the local area with no formal schooling currently available to them due to a lack of available buildings. It seems that the government are able to provide some teachers if the local community have buildings for them to work in. It seems that teachers are cheap to provide, but building materials are not. That's where organisations such as Riley Construction come in.

The food is delicious, and I chat with George about if this is usual. He tells me that it is, and that Nan does a great job of keeping them filled up and content. They generally have a meat option with a mix of rice, potatoes, some vegetables and some fruit. Every couple of days they will have a fish option as well. Of course, it's pretty basic. Luckily no-one has any food allergies, so it's a case of just getting stuck in and enjoying the plain but simple fare. This totally works for me as I am not one that particularly enjoys fancy food in any case. The national dish of Gambia is called Domoda which is meat stewed in peanut puree and served with rice. Another popular dish that Nan offers is Benachin which is meat cooked with rice and vegetables in a tomato-based sauce. To drink there is water, orange juice and baobab juice. Baobab juice is non-alcoholic, packed full of vitamins and probiotics. It's very good for you and can actually be bought in health shops back in the UK. For those that want some alcohol, palm wine is available. The taste and strength varies massively, and I'm warned by George to drink it sparingly.

Most of the men have finished eating now, and Nan collects up the plates. Palm wine is distributed freely, and everyone seems to be settling back and relaxing. One of the English guys brings out a guitar, and one of the locals brings out an instrument which I'm told is called a kora. It's like a large, very-odd shaped guitar which has 21 strings. It makes the most beautiful sound, and the two musicians start striking out uplifting and fun tunes. The combined melodies of the two different instruments are quite amazing, and I'm transfixed by the sound. I lay back on my beanbag and looked up at the stars, listening to the chatter of the men and the lively tunes. I felt happy and content, and as I looked to my side, I saw that James was doing exactly the same thing, whilst George was chatting to some of the other guys.

"Lily, how are you feeling? Are you OK?" asked James.

"Absolutely, I feel surprisingly settled, relaxed and happy," I replied.

"Me too, there is a really homely feel to the camp don't you think?" said James.

"I'm not sure what I was really expecting, but I'm blown away by how welcoming and nice everyone has been," I said.

"I'm so glad that we came. I have a feeling this trip is going to be life-changing," said James.

"You might just be right. I've already realised how lucky and privileged we are in the UK, yet really take it all for granted," I commented.

"Yep," replied James. "I'm totally on board with that feeling."

The next couple of hours passed incredibly quickly. There was some chatting, a lot of laughter, some considerable singing, and quite a bit of palm wine consumed. I did take heed of what George had said though and ensured that I just sipped at it. I could still feel the effect that it was having on my body though, despite drinking probably three times slower than I would at home. I guess it's something completely new for my body to process, so it seems likely that it would have more effect on me than the regular alcohol that I would consume at home.

Soon everything was catching up on me. I yawned, attempting to be discreet, a number of times. But James had noticed. He asked if I was tired, and when I confirmed that I was, he said that he was shattered too and anticipating a long day tomorrow, suggested that we head off to sleep. I stood up, bid farewell to George and the other guys nearby, and James and I headed off towards the tents.

"I'm glad I got a few minutes with you alone before heading to bed," said James.

"Is everything ok?" I asked.

"Absolutely," replied James. "I just wanted to check up on you and make sure you are ok. Are you happy with the sleeping arrangements?"

"Yes, all is good. You are barely twenty feet from me, just some canvas and mosquito nets in between. I'm quite happy, thanks for asking," I replied.

At that James took my hand, pulled me in for a hug, and gave me a quick kiss on the cheek.

"Sleep well, Lily. I'll be thinking of you," said James.

"Thanks," I chuckled. "I'm sure I will. I'll see you in the morning."

I headed off to my tent, grabbed my wash things and headed for the makeshift bathroom which was really just a gazebo. There was water available to rinse your mouth and brush after cleaning your teeth. There were showers, but they were a bit more makeshift and probably only for use in the daytime. The showers consisted of a small walk-in unit with a hose. There was a clip so that you could at least hang the hose up to make everything a bit easier. The unit was three walls and a door. There was no proper floor and no roof. It was hardly The Ritz, but could definitely be a lot worse. The toilets were much the same – units to sit on (chemical toilets) with three walls and a door. Again, no roof or lighting other than the moon.

I completed what I needed to do, and then headed off to my tent. I made sure that the mosquito nets were securely sealed and climbed into my sleeping bag. I felt quite warm and content, and soon drifted off to sleep. Other than waking up a couple of times from various hooting and animal noises, I slept soundly as it had been a very long and draining day.

Chapter 19

It was 7 a.m. when I woke, and I could hear the bustling sounds of the camp. I quickly pulled on some clothes, and then headed outside, making sure to seal up the mosquito nets again. I had slept really well and felt nice and refreshed. After popping to the loo, I wandered over towards the remains of the campfire where people were eating breakfast.

"Morning. What are you eating George?" I asked. He looked like he was eating sweet and sour chicken balls.

"Morning Lily. How are you?" Geoge replied continuing with, "Today's speciality is Akara. It's delightful. It's made with black-eyed peas which are ground into flour and deep-fried. It's with Nan's special sauce and although I have no idea of the ingredients, it's delicious – trust me!".

"Well, it looks great, even if it doesn't really look like something you would normally eat for breakfast," I responded.

"Try it," laughed George. "You'll never look back."

I headed over and nodded to Nan, whilst taking a bowl and helping myself to Akara.

"This looks amazing," I said to Nan. "Thank you so much for taking such good care of us."

"It's a pleasure," replied Nan. "It's just like having an extra big family to look after. I love it."

I picked up some of the baobab juice and a good portion of the Akara. I needed to make sure that I had my fair share before the others started to help themselves to more. Certainly, at dinner last night, absolutely nothing was left over. Everything was devoured down to the last grain of rice.

I turned back to sit beside George. James hadn't yet arrived, but I was assured he would be here imminently. I started to eat and my goodness, the Akara was absolutely delightful. The sauce was amazing, if perhaps just very slightly too spicy for this time of the day for me. But it really was amazing, and I just made sure to wash it down with a good amount of baobab juice. It was really nice to try out the local food and drinks. I'm not the most adventurous when it comes to dining, but this is a totally different experience, and I was definitely making the most of it.

It was already hot. The temperature in Gambia this time of year tends to be around 30 degrees celsius and it was already about 28 degrees at this time in the morning. It felt very hot to me. I was glad that I had taken James' advice and bought a very thin sleeping bag otherwise I would have been roasting. The temperature really doesn't drop that much at night. Gambia is a sub-tropical climate with consistent weather throughout the year. We were just at the end of the dry season, so whilst it had been dry so far, we would most probably get some rainy weather in what they call the 'Green Season' which is July, August and September. However, the rain does tend to come at night, which hopefully means that it won't interrupt the building work too much.

After breakfast, there was a group meeting to start off the day. This took place most mornings to discuss any issues that had risen, to allocate jobs and tasks to people and to co-ordinate things. George was in charge of the meeting and was managing the entire project. Firstly, he allocated the locals into three groups – one was security, one was laying the mud bricks, and one was logistics. This logistics group basically involved fetching and carrying building materials, driving the vehicles that were available and getting things to where they needed to be.

George then explained that James would work with him to go through the plans and discuss the detail and any issues that arose. And the rest of the men from the UK were allocated into two groups, one to work on the main school building and one to work on the grass huts that were also being built. He then turned to me and explained that he needed me to keep a track of the materials that had been delivered, where they had been allocated, when they had been used and what was remaining. He said that it was almost a quantity surveyor type job, but important in that I would be able to predict what building materials we were going to run out of. Also, alongside this, I would keep a report of the costs involved. Oh, and I needed to train up an assistant to carry on the role after I had left.

Whilst much of the costs were being covered by the charity setup by Riley Construction, it was still important that we could report back where the money had been spent and ensure that we were as efficient as possible. Equally, we didn't want to run out of materials that would hold up the job as we were working to very tight deadlines. It was therefore an important role. Up until this point a young man called Omar had been attempting to do the job, but with no official schooling to his name he was struggling somewhat. It had been assigned to me to try and help and educate Omar to get things back on track, and ensure that once I had left, he could keep things going better. It seemed they had already had significant work held up due to a shortage of cement available at the right time and in the right place.

I remember thinking that I wouldn't be very useful when George first mentioned coming out here to help. I had assumed that I would need building and DIY skills. But actually, this was something that I could really get my teeth into. And Omar, despite being quite clueless, was actually very intelligent. He just hadn't had the opportunity to learn when he was growing up. It certainly was not that he wasn't clever. It was just a lack of education. And quite a bit of the role included working with manual spreadsheets. Omar hadn't devised a system to do this and had got into a bit of a pickle. So, my time that first morning was spent doing an inventory with him to find out what materials we currently had available and where they were.

Every few mornings a truck arrived bringing lots of additional materials. There hadn't currently been a system in place to handle this, so that was all going to change now. I got into full-scale planning mode, and started working with Omar to explain what I was doing and why it would help. He quickly grasped what I was trying to achieve, and after we'd finished working the main areas of materials, he took me to other areas where materials had been dumped. By lunchtime, when George returned, we had a pretty detailed inventory of everything available to date. The plan was to sit with George and James and go through the additional materials that we would need to complete the bulk of the building operation.

We soon had a quick break for lunch. Whilst dinner was a drawn out and lengthy affair, lunch was quick and functional. There was too much to do and little time to do it. There was some rice, some bits of meat and lots of bread and banana leaves to make something resembling sandwiches. Plus, the most beautiful tasting tomatoes that I have ever eaten. It's like a completely different species of tomatoes than we get back home. Much of the salad back home has very little taste by the time it makes it onto our plates. The tomatoes here have so much flavour – it's like eating a mouthful of exploding stars.

Omar and I spent the afternoon sitting with George and James, going through the building plans and figuring out what materials we needed, in which order and how quickly. From this, Riley Construction could then organise the sourcing and shipping of those materials. It wasn't possible for large trucks to reach our remote location, so some materials had to be taken from a large truck and split into multiple smaller trucks and Jeeps to get them to their final destination. This also has a large implication on the security team as it's not possible to leave materials unattended or they will disappear. Everything has a value to someone in a country like The Gambia.

We spent many hours mulling over the plans. Omar had already turned into a really important part of the team. Whilst he might have not had much basic education, he was a master when it came to mud bricks, their storage, functionality and capability. Whilst George and James had brilliant engineering minds, they weren't familiar with building with mud bricks, or corrugated roofs for that matter.

By the end of the afternoon, we had the next few weeks of plans all laid out. We knew what we needed and when we needed it by. This had been passed onto Riley Construction so they could sort out their element. We also realised that we needed to have more security people on the days that the deliveries were taking place. We were short on building staff, so it was confirmed that we needed to recruit three more security people to help out on a part-time basis. There were plenty of people that would jump at the chance of some work, so we had no concerns there. And there was enough money in the overspill budget to pay for them.

As for me, well, I had learnt a huge amount. I'm a very organised person, I'm good with numbers and I'm good at devising a process to solve a problem. I realised now that the lack of DIY skills was no issue at all. I finally felt like a really valuable member of the team, and that put a big smile on my face because it had been a primary concern of mine. I hadn't wanted to get in the way of the project, but instead of that, I had become a very valuable team member. It was also enlightening to see both George and James in a totally different light. I'd not thought about either of them from a romantic perspective today, but more like work colleagues. It was really good to see a new side to them. They were both incredibly clever and impressive in how they worked. And the fact that they didn't really know each other either was not evident at all – it seemed like they had been working together all their lives – they seemed so in tune with each other.

I suddenly felt a pang of hunger and looked at my watch. Good gracious – it was gone 6pm. I had no idea how the time had flown. We gathered up the plans and I filed them all carefully in a binder. George thanked us all and told us that he would sleep easier now. It had all been a bit hit and miss up until now, but he felt like things were planned much better moving forwards.

I headed off and had a shower. It felt really good to wash off the dust, dirt and grime of the day. It had been hot, and the humidity was gradually rising, so it felt great to get under the shower (well, hose really). After quickly dressing and a liberal spray of mosquito repellent it was time for dinner.

Tonight's offering from Nan was Fish Yassa. It was beautiful tasting fish with an onion-lemony-mustard type sauce served with rice and vegetables. The food may be fairly basic here, but my goodness it tasted amazing. The fish is apparently Tilapia. I've never heard of it, but it's very common here in Gambia, tastes delicious and is packed full of lean protein and nutrients. I'm not a massive fan of picking out fish bones, but it was worth the effort in this case.

I ate with a group of people which included both George and James. I hadn't really had much of a chance for a one-on-one talk with either of them yet. I hadn't realised quite how long and busy the days were going to be, but I guess with such short timescales we really needed to get on with things.

The next day we had the biggest delivery of materials coming in, so Omar and I would be rushed off our feet, working with the logistics team to get everything inventoried and then distributed accordingly.

As we finished eating, James asked if I wanted to have a stroll just outside the camp with him. He'd been chatting to one of the locals who had told him about a beautiful place to watch the sunset. The sunset tonight was supposed to be at 7:38pm and it was already approaching 7.20pm so we carried our plates over to Nan and then left the camp. I'd seen George had listened to our arrangements, but he hadn't seemed perturbed by the fact that James and I were going out for a walk together. He'd just carried on chatting about the work planned for tomorrow. James had obviously noticed the same thing because he brought it up in conversation as we were walking.

"George didn't seem bothered by us leaving camp for a stroll together," commented James.

"I thought the same thing," I replied. "He really is a laid-back character. When I first suggested that you were interested in coming to Gambia with me, he seemed more pleased with the idea that you would be able to contribute to the project rather than concerned that you might be competition."

"We did have a chat before we left the UK about it actually," responded James.

"Oh, really? I didn't know that," I said. "Tell me more please."

"He facetimed me from the airport when he was flying out here. He said that he did like you and was fully aware that I also liked you. But he just said that he believed in fate, and that if you two were meant to be then it would work out somehow," said James. "I got the impression his primary concern was the project going well, hence he was happy to accommodate me accompanying you on the trip."

"It's quite a refreshing attitude I think," I replied. "And he's right. The more that you push people apart the more they want to be together."

"Well, it's nice to finally get a little alone time with you," said James and he reached out and took hold of my hand.

We walked along quietly for a few minutes. We were walking through a wooded area that appeared to be quite a well used track. The noise of the birds was quite amazing, and I could hear the odd monkey too. I hadn't yet spotted one though. It felt really nice holding James's hand. We seemed to fit together well, and I felt really comfortable with him.

We soon came to the edge of a small ravine. There was an outcrop of rocks and a steep slope down to a large stream.

"This is where I wanted to bring you," said James. "It's a beautiful spot to watch the sunset. Let's sit down on these rocks."

James was right. The sun was starting to dip behind the far side of the ravine and the sky was a spectacular riot of yellow, orange and red colours. James proceeded to tell me that the amazing sunsets in Africa are caused by the high levels of dust in the atmosphere refracting the light from the sun. The sun looks bigger than back in the UK, which I guess makes sense as we are much nearer the equator and therefore nearer to the sun.

We continued to chat, talking about the day's activities, and what the plans were for the next few days. I know that James and George would be very busy on more practical stuff now, rather than the planning day that we had today.

"Can I ask you something, Lily?" asked James.

"Of course," I replied. "What is it?"

"How are you feeling about you and me at the moment?" he asked.

I had a feeling this question was coming. And it was very difficult to answer. Right now, I did not really feel much closer to having an answer for him.

"Well, I love spending time with you, and I'm equally happy doing activities with you or just chilling out together as we are now," I replied.

"Come on Lily, that's not an answer. You know what I mean. Do you feel a spark with me?" asked James.

"I'm scared to lose our friendship," I said. "But I've always found you incredibly attractive, and as I said, I love spending time with you. So yes, the spark is definitely there. I guess the question is more whether I want to act on that spark."

"So do you?" asked James. "What's holding you back?"

"Three things really. The first is that you hurt me the first time around, so it's hard to willingly put myself in a vulnerable position again. The second is that I really value our friendship and I don't want to do anything to jeopardise that. Other than Molly, you are probably my next best friend. Certainly my best male friend," I said.

"That's only two things," said James quietly as I ground to a halt.

"And the third is George. I've had a handful of dates with him, and he is a truly great guy. Plus, I feel like I owe something to him by the fact that I'm here in Gambia right now. He's also been amazing about you accompanying me, and that's not something that most men would be able to handle," I said.

"But don't forget, you literally had only known him a couple of weeks before he came here. And we are also doing him a favour in contributing to the project ourselves," commented James.

"Well, this is true. And whilst he is clearly a great guy and I like his company, I'm not sure how much chemistry there is with him. And that is a fundamental part of a relationship," I mused.

"Can I ask if you have slept with him?" said James. "Or is that a bit personal?"

"It's very personal, but in answer to your question, no, I haven't slept with him," I replied.

James smiled at me, and my answer seemed to put him at ease. I also noticed that it was getting dark very quickly – much more quickly than it does in the UK. I imagine that's because we are so much closer to the equator. I could see a few stars starting to peak out, and I could hear the change in the animal and bird noises.

"Quick, look, over there," whispered James, pointing to a tree visible but almost silhouetted against a reddy black sky. "See the monkeys?"

I strained my eyes in the changing light, and suddenly saw the two monkeys sitting on the lowest bough of the tree. What a fabulous sight, especially with the colours of the sky behind them. I lifted up my phone to take a photo, not sure that I would really be able to capture the moment, but certainly willing to try.

"That's awesome to see the monkeys in the wild," I whispered back.

"Come here," suggested James. He lifted his arm inviting me to snuggle up into his side which I did gratefully. Again, I felt really comfortable being with him. I could feel the warmth emanating from him, and if I rested my head on his chest, I could feel his heart beating – steadily and like a metronome. We sat together, in silence, for quite a few minutes, watching as darkness fell. I felt content, at one with nature and very serene. It was an amazing feeling, and I could recognise the feeling from when I swim in the river. It's the after effect of endorphins flowing. It's a beautiful, natural high.

"People pay a lot of money for this feeling," said James quietly. He was clearly feeling the same as I was, but did clarify by then saying, "the feel good feeling that you get from endorphins, serotonin, oxytocin and dopamine. That's why people take recreational drugs such as cocaine. It releases dopamine in the body in high quantities."

"So, the feeling that I get after running, or swimming in the river, or cuddling up with you, is similar to the high that drug users get from cocaine?" I asked.

"Exactly that," clarified James. "Isn't that amazing?"

"It truly is," I agreed. "Except that I don't have to pay for it, and I can replicate it on a regular basis."

"And that's the thing with drug addiction," said James. "People are always chasing their best high. But as their bodies become used to the drug of choice, cocaine for example, they need to take more and more to get the same effect that they had previously. And that's how addiction happens. And if you don't break the cycle then you keep chasing that high and end up overdosing and maybe even end up dead."

"You seem to know a lot about it," I commented.

"I wish I didn't," said James. "One of my close friends from school became a cocaine addict. And when that didn't give him enough of a buzz, he moved onto even stronger drugs. And later mixing different recreational drugs together. He sadly died of an overdose. He was only twenty-one years old. He was a great guy – and super clever. He even had a PhD in Geology."

"That's so sad James," I said. "I'm so sorry to hear that."

"It really was," said James. "The funeral absolutely broke my heart. There must have been at least 300 friends inside and outside the church as well as his family. It was just awful for such a young man with so much promise to lose his life so unnecessarily. That's why I have no interest in hanging out with anyone that takes drugs now."

"Me neither," I agreed.

By now it was dark, and there were thousands of stars visible.

"Look up James, check out the stars. You can actually see the Milky Way," I commented. "There is so much light pollution back home, that you can rarely get a good view of the stars and the galaxy in which we belong. But here it's amazing."

I lifted my arm and pointed out the thick band of stars which was the view of the Milky Way from the Earth's perspective. Once you understand what you are looking at and open up your mind, it was a truly phenomenal picture.

"That's amazing," said James. "Doesn't the cosmos just make you feel so inconsequential?"

"Here on earth, we really are about as significant as a piece of dust in the grand scheme of things," I agreed. "I once went to a series of lectures on cosmology. I used to come out of those lectures just realising what a tiny, tiny dot Earth is and how insignificant human beings are."

We continued to sit in silence, looking at the sky and occasionally pointing out some of the constellations that we were familiar with. They were in a different place as we were looking at them from a different perspective. Even the moon looked different. It's fascinating really.

"Shall we head back?" suggested James.

We both stood up, shook off our clothes, held hands, and walked slowly back to camp. It was very dark now, so we had to pick our way carefully. We both tripped a couple of times, so I was glad that I was holding James's hand.

As we made it back into camp, we could hear the sounds of the guitar and the kora which were being played again. It was a truly romantic moment and I felt like I was being serenaded. The flames from the campfire were crackling and popping, and we joined the edge of the circle. The next hour was spent chatting happily and quietly while supping on some palm wine. The volume gradually increased as the wine was consumed, and by 10 p.m. there were some raucous laughs and some rather rude jokes and anecdotes being told.

I yawned, not once but twice. And this set James off who was still sitting next to me. It was time for bed. It had been a long day, and we had an even longer one planned for tomorrow. I said goodnight to the rest of the group, and James and I both headed off to get ready for bed.

"I'd love to share your tent with you," suggested James quietly.

"I don't think that's a very good idea, much as I would like to," I replied. "I really don't want to do anything to upset George, and he's been so accommodating and amazing to us. Let's keep the respect."

"You are right Lily," said James. "I apologise. I will attempt to keep my desires in check. George has been amazing, and I don't want to rub his nose in anything."

I bid farewell to James and headed off to bed. I had really, really, really wanted to kiss him, but I was also quite enjoying not acting on my immediate emotions and seeing how things developed. As I settled down in bed, after ensuring the mosquito net was done up perfectly, I pondered how I was feeling. It seemed that trying to keep things in check was just making my feelings for James grow even more. The desire was certainly increasing, I was loving his company, and just wanted to hold him and touch him. I was craving attention from him, and it was giving me an amazing high. I was fairly sure that he was feeling the same too. I wondered if I would fall asleep quickly, but I did, and enjoyed a very pleasant night dreaming about being with James.

Chapter 20

The next day flew by. We had a number of deliveries of materials, so Omar and I were working flat out checking off everything as it arrived and then figuring out the logistics for where it needed to go. We had one large truck arrive in the nearest town, and then had to shuttle all the materials via a small lorry and the Jeeps back to camp. The Jeeps were then used to ferry materials around within camp.

We had a quick stop for lunch and George popped over to talk to me. He wanted the two of us to go out that evening so that we could have a chat. He was going to take me to the nearest town so that we could visit a restaurant. I was looking forward to spending a little one-on-one time with George and also have a meal out. I was a little concerned that I didn't have anything nice to wear, but George put me at ease, and said there weren't any restaurants in this part of Gambia that require anything other than casual clothes. He said that in Banjul and Serekuna, there are some high-class restaurants, but in the rural areas of Gambia it's all very low key.

Later that evening, as everyone else started to gather around the fire, George and I hopped into the Jeep that he had commandeered. As we bounced and lurched away from camp, George explained that we would be travelling for about half an hour to find a decent restaurant. He wanted me to experience some true Gambian food, but a little less basic than we had been eating at camp.

The conversation on route was nice and relaxed. George was telling me how things were going in the main school building and explained that the construction of the grass huts would be running in parallel as and when manpower was available. This week and next week had the most volunteers, and after that, the number of people available to work would gradually reduce. Whilst he was happy with the pace of construction so far, he did need the bulk of the structural work to get completed while the resources were still available. He said again how thankful he was to have the additional expertise from James. I was starting to feel that George and James had a bit of a bromance going on, such was their mutual enjoyment of each other's company.

Reflecting upon the two of them, they definitely share a number of characteristics. They are both driven, adventurous, determined and gain great pleasure out of helping others. They have a similar streak of empathy and kindness whilst still being strong and supportive.

We soon arrived at the neighbouring town. Like most areas it was a contrast between the nicer parts and the very poor parts. As we approached in the Jeep, the inevitable string of children ran behind us, holding out their hands and shouting for sweets. As we pulled to a stop they crowded behind us, and George pulled a bag of sweets out of the glove compartment.

"Here Lily, you'd best give them this. Just make it clear that's all we have," he suggested.

I did as he said and distributed the sweets to each of the children. As they asked for more, I shook my head and said "No more, no more. All gone." I'm not sure how much English they understood, but they seemed to get the gist at least.

George jumped out, walked around the Jeep, and grabbed my hand. He had managed to park directly outside the restaurant which was called Calypso. The restaurant was set back from the road and was structured like a thatched gazebo. There was a fully stocked bar with a smart looking bartender, and then around twenty tables with several waiters carrying drinks and food. The majority of the tables were already full, and the diners comprised of mainly white people with a few locals. George told me that there were quite a few ex-pats that lived in the area, mainly here to help build the communities. Some were here permanently but most were temporary.

The atmosphere tonight was buzzing and friendly. The food that was being carried around by the waiters looked absolutely sensational, and my mouth was watering. I felt really happy and relaxed, and it was nice to get a chance to spend time with George alone.

George ordered us a bottle of sparkling wine called Silverthorn which is made in South Africa. Our waiter told us that it is made using the Cap Classique method. Ostensibly, it's the same process as making Champagne, and I agreed that the final taste was much the same. It was delicious and went down far too smoothly.

The streets outside the restaurant were bustling and crowded, even at this time of the evening. But the ambience inside the restaurant was pleasant and relaxed. As we sipped on our sparkling wine, I consulted George on what to order.

"I have an idea, Lily. Let me speak to the waiter a moment," said George beckoning to the nearest staff member.

"Excuse me, my friend Lily here has never been to a Gambian restaurant before. Rather than sticking to the main menu, would it be possible to have a sample of maybe three or four local dishes please?" George asked with a twinkle in his eye.

"That sounds like an excellent suggestion sir," said the waiter. "Let me check with the kitchen a moment." The waiter headed towards the back of the restaurant.

"That's a brilliant idea, George, I hope they will accommodate us," I nodded enthusiastically.

"They are very good here, and will try to provide what you ask if they are able," said George.

A few minutes later the waiter returned.

"Sir, we can accommodate your request. The cost will be 3,500 dalami plus the wine," said the waiter. "Would you like to proceed?"

"Yes please, and thank you for being so helpful," said George.

The waiter then told us that his name was John and that he would be looking after us tonight.

"I assume his name isn't really John," I commented to George once the waiter has disappeared.

"No, most probably not," agreed George. "They tend to pick English names if they have names that wouldn't be recognised by an English person. That way they are more relatable, and likely to earn more tips."

"That make sense," I mused.

We continued to chat in a light-hearted manner. George was entertaining me with funny stories about things that had happened on camp – both this year and in previous years. It seemed no time at all before the waiter returned with a selection of dishes which he explained as he placed them on the table.

The first plate that he placed down was Afra. This was effectively grilled beef served on a bed of onions with seasoning. The second option I recognised as we had eaten it at camp. It was called Yassa Ganarr. This is chicken with onions, peppers, seasoning, salt, lime and mustard.

Next up was white Benachin which is a simple dish of chicken cooked with oil, onions, garlic, pepper, tomato, carrots, seasoning, cassava, and bay leaves. Finally, we had

Akara which looks like breaded balls. Akara is made with black eye peas and salt, and it is served with a sauce of onions, habanero and chilli peppers, salt, and Maggi. Maggi is like a stock cube and gives additional, well balanced flavours. Akara can be served for breakfast, or with more flavouring, for evening meal.

George and I shared the food, and after about thirty minutes I was totally full. We had polished off much of the delicious tasty offerings, and I felt like could hardly move. George had commented that he was quite impressed that I could finish such a substantial amount of food yet remain so slight. I wasn't quite sure if that was a compliment or not but decided not to dwell on it.

The waiter cleared away the remains of our feast, and we finished off the bottle of Silverthorn. George asked me if I wanted any more, but I just asked for some water. I was that full that I didn't think I could even accommodate any more wine.

"There is one more thing for us to eat," said George.

"Really? I'm not sure I could eat another thing," I replied.

"You will appreciate this," laughed George.

As the waiter approached, George asked for something called Chakri. When I asked what it was, he explained that it is a very traditional dessert made from couscous mixed with yoghurt. It can have various other ingredients added, depending on the region where it's made. Here they add pineapple, which sounded fabulous.

When the Chakri arrived, I took my first mouthful a little hesitantly. But I needn't have worried. It was like an explosion of flavour and sensation in my mouth. It was truly delicious. I was so grateful to George for taking the time to bring me out of camp and give me a true Gambian restaurant experience. It was such a thoughtful thing to do, and I was extremely grateful.

A short while later, George settled up with the waiter, gave a tip and we left the restaurant. We headed back to the Jeep, although George asked if I minded taking a detour on the way back.

"Where are we heading?" I asked. Even though I was enjoying the adventure, I was starting to feel tired.

"There is a part of the River Gambia just a few miles from here which is truly remote and stunning. I'd love to take you there so we can sit and have a chat for a little bit," replied George. "Is that ok?"

"Of course, it sounds lovely," I agreed.

Fifteen minutes later we bounced off the road and made our way down a really rough track through a wooded area. I wasn't sure it had any resemblance to a road, and it felt like we were driving into the middle of nowhere. However, just a couple of minutes later we broke out of the trees and in front of us I could see the river. Although it was a dark night, it was clear, and the moonlight was very bright once we had emerged from under the trees.

"Let's go," said George, reaching into the back of the Jeep and grabbing a couple of blankets.

We walked for just a couple of minutes and found a rocky outcrop on the edge of the river. George laid out the blankets, took my hand, and requested that I sit. As he settled next to me, he asked if I could hear the monkeys.

As I listened carefully, I could indeed hear some clattering noises and an odd sound that resembled a baby scream.

"Is that the monkeys?" I asked quietly.

"Yes, that's right. They make loads of different sounds. I love listening to them."

Suddenly I heard something totally different.

"Is that a cow?" I asked.

"Yes," laughed George. "There are a lot of cows around here".

"How about crocodiles?" I asked. "Are we likely to get attacked by a crocodile?"

"There are lots of crocodiles here, but it's quite rare for them to attack. I think we will be safe," laughed George.

"Not sure it's really a laughing matter," I replied nervously. "Now I've thought about it, I can't get it out of my head."

"I'll look after you, Lily. Don't worry."

We continued chatting. George sat closer to me and put his arm around me, and I snuggled into it.

"So how are you feeling?" George asked.

"I'm feeling very grateful to be here," I replied. "It's amazing to have the opportunity to come to Gambia. I'm so happy."

"That wasn't quite what I meant," replied George. "I guess I was asking how you feel about me, and how you are feeling about James?"

I turned and scrutinised George closely. It was a question I had been asking myself a lot recently. It's difficult to answer, because I don't really know. Both men have so many positives going for them, but of course I don't have any history with George. We have only met a handful of times, while I have known James for some time – and of course we did date for a few weeks a couple of years back.

"It's really difficult to answer," I explained. "I've known James for a couple of years, and of course we did date for a good few weeks. But then we've just been friends ever since, so it's quite strange to be thinking of him in a different light. But then you came along, and I've really enjoyed getting to know you. So, I'm quite confused in all honesty."

There were a couple of minutes silence, but it wasn't awkward at all. I didn't feel the need to say anything further, and just waited to see how George would reply.

"I've also cherished getting to know you, Lily," replied George. "You are a truly beautiful person, inside and out. You are fun, adventurous, charismatic and also easy-going. It's a wonderful combination of characteristics." George stopped speaking, but I didn't think he had finished.

"I'm not sure how much chemistry there is between us. I don't think we've spent enough time together to determine if we have an amazing friendship, or if there really is a big enough spark between us. I've been around the block enough times to know that chemistry is really important – and you can't change it. It has to be there, at least to some extent, from the start," George said.

I felt this massive sense of relief because this is exactly how I feel. It was like a weight had been removed from my shoulders.

"That's how I feel," I agreed quietly. "I absolutely love spending time with you, and I have enjoyed kissing you, but I haven't had the urge to rip your clothes off – not yet at least."

George laughed and gave me a big hug.

"I've been watching your interactions with James, and aside from the fact that you clearly have a great friendship with him, there does seem to be something more there. Or that's what it looks like from an outsider's perspective anyway. When you talk with James, your face lights up, and his does the same. I can see you watching him when you aren't with him. And the two of you seem to be magnetically attracted to each other. He's a great guy, and you're a great girl and I don't want to stand in the way of that." This time George seemed to have finished.

"I've been very wary and wanting to keep my options open. And that's because I felt second best after he chose to go back to his original girlfriend, Jasmine, just a few weeks after we started dating the first time around. I was hurt, and this time I think self-preservation has kicked in. I'm scared of being hurt again. I know he wouldn't do it intentionally, and it wasn't deliberate – I understand why he did what he did. But it was just bad timing really. But it does mean that I have my defences up."

"Can I give you some advice?" asked George.

"Please do," I replied. "I have a lot of respect for you, and I would appreciate hearing your thoughts."

"Follow your heart. Don't be afraid. I know it's hard, especially with your shared history, but it's obvious that he genuinely likes you, and he is a truly good person. And I think the feelings are reciprocated. I think he's a great guy. Despite the fact that he's clearly going to steal my girl…" George laughed before he carried on. "I don't think that I can compete with him to be honest. I think I've missed the boat. Maybe if I'd met you a few months ago, but I think, once you admit it, you will realise how much you like him. I think you've just been fighting it, and perhaps using me as a bit of shelter from your feelings, rather than facing the reality of the situation. Does that make sense?"

"It does make sense, and I think you might be right. I have to say though, this really does emphasise what an amazing man you are," I agreed. "There are not many men mature enough to handle this situation as well as you have."

"It is what it is," said George. "It's clear to me that you are still into James. And I really don't want to get embroiled in that situation and end up hurt when you finally wake up and realise the extent of your feelings for him. It's better off that we just have a great friendship, and you and James crack on. If you didn't, I really feel that you would spend the rest of your life wondering 'what if'."

I laid back and looked at the stars and thought about it. Now that I had acknowledged my feelings, I realised how right George is. And I know that James has a lot of feelings for me too. I just hadn't been open to them. The talk with George had done me the world of good, and I felt relieved.

"Come on," said George jumping up and offering me his hand. "Let's head back to camp."

I took hold of George's hand and allowed him to pull me up.

"Thank you, George. I'm truly grateful. I hope we will always be friends," I said.

"I hope that too," replied George. "And I think we will be. At least I know I get on well with your future boyfriend." And with that George laughed and we walked back to the Jeep and headed back to camp.

Chapter 21

After the chat with George, I was excited to get back to camp and see James. It was bizarre, but although I didn't need George's approval, somehow, what he said had really made me positive about moving forward with James. I felt that George and I had a truly wonderful friendship, but I never had been quite convinced how much chemistry there was between us. And chemistry is essential in a relationship. Of course, feelings grow naturally as you get to know someone in more depth, but there has to be that initial spark.

The first time around, the spark with James had been immense. And I think that was why it had taken me so long to open up to James and allow the fire to reignite. It's natural that walls come up after you have been rejected, and although James had always said that our original relationship was just bad timing, naturally, it still felt like rejection to me.

However, perhaps it's possible that James is the one. The one that I could settle down and be happy with. And having known him for quite some time now, I am already fully onboard with the fact that he is a loyal, hardworking, ambitious, kind and adventurous person. If I had to write a wanted list for my future partner, I really could be writing about James.

Now that things were officially closed down with George, I felt like I should take that chance, and crack on with James. I was excited to talk to him again.

Thirty minutes later George parked up, and we headed towards the campfire, only to find that it was very quiet. There were only three people left huddled around the fire, clearly the rest had gone to bed. I hadn't realised how much time had passed, and it was actually quite late. I'd have to wait until tomorrow to talk to James.

After being rather excited, it did take me a little while to fall asleep, but the next thing I knew the birds were cheeping again and I woke up in my rather warm tent. The temperature must be mid-twenties already and it was only around seven am.

As I stuck my head out of my tent, I spotted James emerging from his. I beckoned him over, and James crawled into my tent to join me.

"How was your evening last night Lily?" asked James. "I missed you."

I gazed into his beautiful eyes and smiled. He looked a bit hesitant and unsure of himself. I guess that we had returned late, so he would have no idea about how I was feeling.

"It was good thank you. George took me to a really great restaurant, and we had a good, long chat," I replied.

"I waited up for a while, but you must have been quite late back," said James.

"We had a lot to talk about," I said.

"So, are you going to give me a rundown, or are you going to leave me in suspense?" asked James.

I laughed and reached for his hand.

"George and I agreed that we are great friends, and that we are both very happy with that," I said quietly.

"Well, that's a relief," said James. "I wasn't quite sure how you felt about him as he is clearly a great guy."

"He is a good man, and I'm so grateful to have him as a friend. After all, if I hadn't met him, we wouldn't have been on this adventure," I replied.

"So, what does this mean for us?" asked James.

"Well, I'm really excited about us," I said. "I feel like we have a chance to start afresh, with no distractions and no reason to feel guilty about anything."

"What bloody fantastic news," said James. "Come here please."

James pulled gently on my arm, and I cuddled up next to him.

"Are we finally going to get the timing right now?" chuckled James.

"Well, maybe things do align in the end," I agreed.

"And George is really ok with this?" asked James.

"Yes, he is. In fact, he gave us his blessing. He said it was clear that we had feelings for each other, and he didn't want to confuse things or get in the way," I confirmed.

"Well, that's really made my day. Or maybe my week. Or even the year?" debated James.

I felt so happy. It seemed that making this decision had taken a weight off my shoulders and I was really happy to explore a relationship with James. Whilst I had initially been hesitant, now that I had embraced and moved on from our shared history, I felt really excited to see where things would go.

James lay back against the pillow and pulled me into his body. I snuggled up and wedged in the crook of his arm. We lay comfortably together, and just enjoyed the moment. James rolled part way onto his side, and his lips reached for mine. As our lips came together, I savoured the moment. It had been a long time coming and it felt amazingly natural and exciting to be kissed by him again. He kissed me softly and I felt his tongue slide into my mouth. I felt the butterflies in my stomach flutter, and I sighed softly.

"Bored already?" laughed James.

"Hardly," I answered. "Truthfully, it's amazing to kiss you again. I've been dying to do that."

"Well, you kept that quiet," murmured James. "You could have put me out of my misery a bit earlier."

"I didn't mean to tease you. It just took me some time to work out what I wanted," I said. "My defences were up after what happened last time around, but you've gradually chipped away at them, and I think they have entirely collapsed now."

"That makes me indescribably happy," replied James. "It's so good to have you in my arms again."

"I don't want to shove it in George's face though. I think we need to respect his feelings and keep a lid on things until we get back home," I suggested.

"I agree, he really has been amazingly good about everything, so I don't want to rub it in. I'm sure he would rather you are in his arms really, so we need to be considerate and respectful," agreed James.

"I'm so glad that we are on the same page. I think the three of us will have a great friendship moving forwards," I said.

We continued to chat for a few more minutes until we really had to get up. Aside from the fact that we had work to do, it was also getting rather hot and uncomfortable inside the tent. James climbed out first then held out his hand to help pull me up and out of the tent.

After a quick breakfast, we were back to work. We had more deliveries coming, so Omar and I were busy. And James and George were cracking on with the erection of the roof panels as the sides of the main building were complete. George was delighted with the progress of the build. It seems that having the materials properly organised was helping immensely, and the addition of James's expertise had helped to speed things up considerably. Both James and I felt very proud that we had a significant impact on the project, even in just a week or so.

Chapter 22

The next week passed by at what felt like the speed of light. We got into a good routine at the camp, and other than a few evening walks, James and I just enjoyed the company of the rest of the team around the campfire on the evenings. We were incredibly busy during the day, and I had also started driving one of the Jeeps to and from the nearest town if we ran out of anything that was holding up the project. I was very proud of how much contribution Omar was now able to make. He was totally invested in ensuring that everything was catalogued and distributed exactly as required which prevented unnecessary wastage. The system that I had put in place, and his attention to detail meant that once James and I left, the process would continue to work. The whole project team was working together smoothly and efficiently, and the results were evident to see in the speed in which the buildings were being constructed.

When it came to bedtime, James and I were desperate to share, but out of respect for George we resisted the temptation. It meant that the feelings between us were hotting up and up and I literally couldn't take my eyes off him. Despite having given us his blessing, I think George was pleased that we weren't cracking on too much in front of him. It was clear that James and I were together, but we refrained from too much affection in public. After all, we would be heading back to the UK in a few days in any case, so we didn't have too long to wait.

James and I had arranged to spend our final day exploring a little of Gambia, before heading back to the airport. George had kindly said that we could borrow a Jeep, and we would be able to leave it in Banjul when we flew home, and he would collect it later that day. That really was incredibly kind of him, but he said it was a thank you for the hard work and massive contribution that we had made to the building project.

So, early in the morning on our penultimate day, we said goodbye to everyone after breakfast, and left camp in the trusty Jeep. James and I cherished the unforgettable memories we had made, and I was sad to be leaving to go home. We had made some truly lifelong friends in the couple of weeks that we had been here. I guess that's what happens when you are thrown into such close proximity with fellow workers. Conversely, I was excited for our final day of exploring.

We were heading to Bakau which is not far from Banjul, where the airport is located. The main place I wanted to visit was Kachikally crocodile pool. I had read up on this attraction and was desperate to visit. The journey there took us nearly three hours, as I insisted that we stopped each time we encountered a cluster of monkeys. It was a beautiful day, hot but devoid of any wind. On one occasion, we parked up in a dense area of woodland and took a little walk. The first thing that we saw was a really pretty green chameleon. We soon turned back though when we encountered a rather large snake. We think it was a puff adder, as it looked like an adder and it did appear to rear at us and 'puff up' when we startled it. To be honest, I'm not sure who was more scared, us or the snake. Needless to say, we hightailed it back to the Jeep and carried on driving. Shortly after this episode we did see a pack of hyenas. They really do sound like a baby laughing.

We finally arrived at Kachikally crocodile pool. I wasn't really sure what to expect, but there must have been well over 80 crocodiles. It seemed that they kept them well fed, so they are all incredibly lazy. There were quite a few other visitors, and although it's not advisable, there is one area where you can touch some of the crocodiles. I was rather nervous but did give one a quick touch.

The Kachikally crocodile pool is known to be a sacred site that is believed to have mystical and healing powers. The origins of these beliefs dates back centuries. According to folklore, the pool was discovered by a holy man who was guided by a dream to find a sacred body of water inhabited by crocodiles. When he found the pool, the crocodiles living there were peaceful and unthreatening. Of course, now the crocodiles are specifically kept well fed to keep them as docile as possible. They are accustomed to humans now so don't feel any threat from them.

The waters of the pool are said to possess curative properties. The locals believe that bathing in or drinking water from the pool can help many ailments including skin conditions, specific physical issues and infertility. Many women who struggle to conceive have visited the pool and the crocodiles.

The crocodiles themselves are revered as guardians of the pool and are considered sacred. They are treated with great respect by the local community – they believe them to be protectors of the site. As a result, harming or disrespecting them could result in misfortune or illness. I was really happy to find out that the numbers of crocodiles in the pool are regularly topped up by crocodiles that are found sick or injured in the wild.

I was fascinated to learn that most of the crocodiles live for 50 to 60 years. The locals told us that the oldest crocodile at Kachikally is reputed to be 80 years of age. That's just incredible and I had no idea that they lived that long. Of course, at Kachikally, they are well fed, protected and have no predators, so they get to live to a ripe old age compared to crocodiles in the wild.

We spent quite some time at the crocodile pool. We were both fascinated to be in such close proximity to them, and for there to be such a relaxed atmosphere. We sat together just watching them, not that there was much movement from the majority of them. James took hold of my hand, and sat next to me, drinking in the experience.

"It's phenomenal isn't it Lily," said James.

"I've been trying to think of the right word to describe this, and the best I can come up with is that it's an ethereal experience," I replied.

"That's a great word to describe it," agreed James. There were a few minutes of comfortable silence.

"There is something that I'd like to ask you, Lily," said James.

"Of course, ask me anything," I answered.

"I'm not sure how this is really supposed to happen in the modern world of dating, but would you please be my girlfriend?" asked James.

I turned slightly to look at James. He looked deep into my eyes, and appeared to be drinking me in. I felt the warmth flowing from him and enveloping me. It really was a very simple answer.

"Yes James. It's an absolute yes. I would love to be your girlfriend," I grinned.

"Thank goodness for that," James replied and leaned over for a kiss. "I was really nervous about asking you."

"Well, I'm really glad that you did," I answered.

James took out his phone to take some pictures of us. We found a kindly tourist who took some photos of the two of us together. Selfies don't always do things justice. It was nice to commemorate the moment with some decent pictures.

"I don't suppose many people get asked to be someone's girlfriend witnessed by a bunch of crocodiles," I laughed.

"It's certainly a unique occasion. It will be hard to forget that's for sure," replied James.

After we finished our visit at the crocodile pool, we headed into Bakau to discover the Craft Fair. What an experience that was. The Gambians are certainly into bartering, and there is every conceivable item that you could possibly want to buy at this thriving and busy market.

Almost every stall holder, and person walking around with their wares, tried to engage with us. It was frantic and exhausting. I enjoyed holding James's hand whilst checking out everything that was on offer. One stall holder tried to persuade James to swap me for a rather nice looking digital camera. It seemed that James was actually quite tempted in this trade, and although he was joking, I wasn't quite clear if the Gambian man was joking or not. In my mind it was time to leave.

George had told us that all the local fishing boats returned to shore around about four pm each day, and then a thriving fish market takes place. He said it was something that shouldn't be missed, so even though we had no intention of buying any fish, we headed off to where the fishing boats docked.

I had never seen quite so many people aboard the boats. It was amazing that they could still float. The majority of the boats were maybe thirty feet long in length, narrow and often carried twenty people as well as all the nets and fish. The catch was brought to shore and tens of stalls were set up with the amazing fish and shellfish on offer. Many of the fish were a good two or even three feet long.

Some of the sellers offered cooked samples, and these were delicious. We sampled a few different types, and the tastes were varied. I wasn't so keen on the very strong fishy-tasting samples, but prefer the more bland types. James thought it hilarious that I preferred the fish that tasted more like chicken than fish. What could I say to that? What I couldn't quite believe though, were the colourful scenes, the loud, vibrant market and how busy it was. It was like an assault on your senses – your ears, your eyes and your tastebuds all at once. There were all different types of fish available, some of which I recognised and many of which I didn't. I was told there were Snappers, Mackerel, Catfish, Bonga Fish and Captain Fish. It was quite an education coming to a market like this.

All in all, we had a thoroughly enjoyable day. It was really fun to absorb the delights of Gambia. I enjoyed meeting a lot of the locals, especially the traders in the markets who were fun, even if rather persistent. However, we were getting rather tired, and I was starting to feel incredibly hungry. Aside from a few samples at the market, we hadn't eaten anything significant all day, so it was time to find a restaurant. We had earlier checked into to our hotel for the night, the Tropic Garden Hotel and attached to that hotel was a reputable restaurant called the House of Flavour. The restaurant served African, European, Chinese and Indian food.

We settled down with a bottle of white Pearly Bay wine and two glasses. We were a little early for dinner, but we planned to have a drink before eating in any case. We also asked for a bottle of water as we were both feeling rather dehydrated after our incredibly busy day. I cuddled up next to James on a sofa and he put his arm around me. Already, it felt really natural to be in a couple with James. My previous concern that sometimes switching from a friendship to something more had been totally allayed. In fact, I now found that concern hilarious, because I couldn't get enough of James. He exuded a magnetic charm, drawing me irresistibly to him.

I found myself constantly longing to touch him. If I was standing next to him, I yearned to hold his hand. If I was sitting next to him, I craved the touch of my leg against his. If we were talking, I couldn't help but stare into his captivating eyes. This feeling is of lust, and with James it was immensely powerful. After a period of growing familiarity and suppressing my feelings for him, it seemed as though emotions had erupted within me like a sudden explosion.

"How are you feeling Lily?" asked James. "It's been an amazing day."

"It has been truly fabulous, and I have enjoyed every single second of it," I replied. "Exploring Gambia has been wholly satisfying and I have loved sharing the adventure with you."

"May it be the start of many adventures that we have together," agreed James.

"Goodness, I hope so," I said. "I feel so happy that we are finally together, it seems like fate finally intervened."

"I am really excited for our future together. It seemed that we could never get the timing right before, but finally, things seem to have worked out for us. Long may it last," said James.

"I can't wait to tell Molly all about it," I laughed. "I've never gone this long without speaking to her before."

"I have no doubt that her and Harry will be absolutely delighted for us, and it will be so fabulous to double-date with them again like we did once before," commented James.

"It does feel so right for us to be together," I agreed. "Whilst I'm super happy to be here, I'm also excited to go home and start real life with you."

"Do you think your mum will be happy for us?" asked James.

"Definitely," I replied. "Mum has always had a soft spot for you. I think she was as disappointed as I was when we split up previously. It was that time that you brought flowers for her when we first started dating. She was blown away by that, and thought you were a keeper for being that thoughtful."

"Well, that's reassuring to hear. I know how important your mum is to you, so I'm glad that I get the seal of approval," replied James.

"You aren't wrong. If my mother took exception to you, it would definitely factor in my decision making. My mother is an amazing woman, and a great judge of character and I have the utmost respect for her."

"Sir, Madam, would you care to accompany me to your table?" asked a waiter that was hovering.

We jumped up and headed into the main area of the restaurant itself. We were presented with menus and the waiter kindly brought the rest of our water and wine over for us. We had been rather slack at drinking so far, we'd tackled more of the water than anything else.

After perusing the menus, we placed our orders. James fancied some Indian while I stuck to a simple Gambian dish which consisted of chicken, chips and salad. I'm not sure how traditional chips really are, but I was happy to go with that selection, after eating mainly Gambian cuisine for the last two weeks. However, the waiter did say that western influences had made chips a core part of the modern Gambian diet, even though previously it would have been mainly rice based. He told us that this is especially the case in the towns and cities, less so in the rural communities.

We had a truly delightful meal. The service was excellent, the food was fantastic and the atmosphere in the now busy restaurant was buzzing. Every day that I spent with James, I could feel us becoming closer, and I was loving the intimacy of this beautiful restaurant after our camp lifestyle of the last two weeks.

A couple of hours later James settled the bill and we headed to our hotel room. There was an amazing looking swimming pool, but we were tired, very full and not really in the mood for swimming. We didn't have an early flight, so we decided we would have a swim before breakfast in the morning. We didn't need to set off for the airport until mid-morning, so we had plenty of time.

We bypassed the hotel bar and headed straight for our room. We'd had such a brilliant time, and after the intense build up of our feelings over the last couple of weeks, I was desperate to get some truly alone time with James. And I felt confident that was what he also desired. As we went up in the lift, James grabbed my hand, pulled me to him and kissed me deeply. The butterflies were hurtling around in my stomach, and I couldn't wait to get more of him. He pushed me up against the side of the lift, and I could feel the growing bulge in his trousers. Sadly, the lift pinged as the hotel was only three floors in total. As we left the lift, James pulled me along the corridor, both of us giggling under our breath. James opened the room with our keycard and pushed me into it, keeping hold of me until we both fell onto the bed.

Such was the build up between us, I felt like I couldn't get enough of him. He kissed me deeply, while tearing off my clothes almost frantically. His got thrown on the floor immediately afterwards and I made sure that his socks joined them. There is nothing so off-putting as a naked man in socks. He pulled me into his arms and it felt so amazing to kiss him and feel our bodies entwined together. He pulled away a moment and took a few deep breaths. I asked if he was ok, and he assured me he was, but that he wanted to savour the moment, not speed through it.

My heart rate eased, and we reined ourselves in a little. He peppered a spray of kisses from my mouth to my ear, down my neck and onto my collarbone. He gently caressed my breasts and bent down to kiss them and lick my nipples. I could feel my nerves twanging, and sensations travelled from my nipples all the way down my body to my toes. I felt like a highly tuned guitar that was being played by an incredible musician.

I felt James's mouth roam over my whole body. He kissed me everywhere from my legs, inside my thighs, across my stomach, across my breasts. He gently navigated my whole body, whilst using his to manoeuvre me as he desired. He spread my legs apart and I could feel a throbbing sensation starting from my very inner core. I had never felt quite so in tune with a man as I did with James. Of course, it wasn't the first time we had slept together. We'd had amazing sex several times when we dated previously. That prior knowledge, the intimacy and the growing desire turned our sex into true lovemaking.

There was certainly no need for lubrication. James's fingers and shortly after, his tongue made me considerably moist within seconds and he soon reached for his jeans to pull on a condom. I was desperate to feel him inside me. James was well endowed and incredibly hard, and I couldn't wait for penetration. We lay on our side as he slowly entered me, and my stomach exploded with butterflies as he pushed steadily until I felt entirely filled up by him. His shaft was incredibly hard and satisfying, and I made sure to match his movements so that he wasn't driving too deep inside me.

As my body accommodated his hardness, I braced against him allowing him to push deeper still. The feelings that rattled around my entire body were so intense. I felt like we had been building up to this moment for months, and it did not disappoint. We moved in synchrony like a couple who had been dancing together for decades. We instinctively seemed to know what worked for each other, and our desire to satisfy each other was overwhelming.

I could feel a climax beginning to build in both of us and our movements quickened. I thought that James was getting close to orgasm as his breathing had becoming rapid and he was quietly moaning. He reached down with his hand and slid his fingers onto my clit, almost immediately tipping me over the edge to orgasm. I clung to his damp, sweaty body, breathing in his personal fragrance as my climax took over my body at the same time as his. We came together and swiftly collapsed onto the bed hardly moving and breathing deeply. That was incredible. I felt truly satiated and now just wanted to sleep in his arms.

James manoeuvred himself so that he could safely retrieve the condom. He stepped briefly into the bathroom and then returned and gathered me up into his arms. The air conditioning was whirring away, and the cool air circulating felt amazing on our damp, sweaty bodies. Our breathing and heart rates gradually returned to normal. I felt incredibly happy, tired, and just wanted to rest. I lay in James's arms, with my head on his chest, listening to the hypnotic and rhythmic beating of his heart. Within minutes both James and I were fast asleep wrapped up together, and there we stayed for many hours.

Chapter 23

We both slept deeply, not waking until gone 7.30 a.m. the next morning. It was the first time that we had slept in a proper bed and a sensible temperature for quite some time. I woke up feeling immensely happy, satisfied and joyful. I wasn't particularly relishing the journey home, but James and I had experienced the most incredible adventure over the last two weeks. I would be pleased to return home for a rest.

James turned to me and kissed me deeply. Such was our desire, that we soon enjoyed another love-making session. And after a brief rest, I was ready to go again, but James pulled away laughing.

"Lily, you have knackered me out. I'm starving, and we wanted to go for a swim before breakfast. We haven't got that long before we need to leave, so we need to get moving. Come on woman. You'll have to wait to savage me again," he laughed.

"Really?" I grumbled. "Are you turning me down already?"

James grabbed my hand and pulled me up from the bed.

"No, I'm not turning you down at all. I'm just hitting the pause button," he insisted.

James handed me my bikini and a towel, and I slipped on the two-piece and wrapped the towel around me. James pulled on some swim trunks, and we headed downstairs to the pool. The pool was outside and felt very warm in comparison to English rivers. It was a decent sized pool that you could actually swim some lengths in. We draped our towels over a sunbed, and jumped into the water. We both relaxed into some lengths, before we enjoyed an embrace and a deep kiss.

We stayed in the water for a good twenty-five minutes, swimming a little, playing a little, kissing a little. We even had a few races across the length of the pool. It seemed that James could beat me at front crawl but couldn't keep up with me in breaststroke. We finished off with an underwater competition, to see who could swim the furthest. James went first and managed a length underwater which I knew would be hard to beat. But I have always been incredibly determined, and even though my lungs were threatening to burst, I managed to complete the length, turnaround and push off the wall, before surfacing three or four strokes later. James was quite impressed at the competence of my swimming, and I delighted in his praise.

We decided that it was time for breakfast, so we retrieved our towels and headed back to our room for a shower and change. We briefly shared the shower, but I preferred the water hotter than James did, so he quickly jumped out, and by the time I had finished washing my hair, he was dressed and ready to go. I quickly got ready, left my hair brushed but wet and we headed down to breakfast. The choice was continental breakfast or a buffet which included much of your traditional English foods. The hotel was clearly used by westerners, so we enjoyed our first Full English in a couple of weeks. We were both starving, so made the most of the buffet, returning a couple of times for additional toast and drinks. Finally, satiated and happy we headed back to our room.

"Have we time for some hanky-panky?" I asked.

James burst out laughing.

"What decade were you born in?" he asked. "You must have been born in about the 1950's to talk about hanky-panky. But the answer is no, we need to be checked out and leaving in the next ten minutes. So, you will just have to contain your desire for the moment."

We gathered together our belongings and quickly checked out of the hotel. It was time to jump in the Jeep and navigate to the airport in Banjul. We had arranged to leave the Jeep in the airport carpark, and the key with a service desk, whereupon George would collect it. Everything went to plan, save for a little navigating through Banjul, and we were sitting in the departures lounge a couple of hours later.

"Are you happy to be returning home?" asked James.

"Well, we have had a truly memorable experience. I'm delighted to be returning coupled up with you, although the thought of going back to work is a little off-putting. But I can't wait to tell Molly and mum about our adventures," I replied. "How about you?"

"I'm truly knackered," replied James. "But also genuinely happy. I'm so happy to have you as my girlfriend now."

We spent the next few minutes laughing at how complicated young people seem to make this dating process. Most people in their twenties seem to go out with someone many times, then they become exclusive, and then a later step is to become boyfriend and girlfriend. Personally, I don't really understand the difference between being exclusive and being in a couple. But equally, I don't really care. I'm just happy to be with James and it feels right to be together. I'm truly content that he feels the same about me.

"I feel like once we get off the plane, we are starting the next chapter of our lives," I commented to James.

"I know exactly how you feel. That's how it seems to be for me too. And I'm just happy that this next chapter, and hopefully the rest of them too, we will tackle together," agreed James. "The Gambian adventure might be over, but I wonder what the next chapter will bring?"

The next few minutes were quiet, and I rested against James gratefully. I truly felt that together, we could tackle the world. At least, after a few days sleep and recovery.

About the Author

Tanya Knight, born in Gloucestershire and now residing in Boston, Lincolnshire, is a dynamic author whose vibrant characters often reflect her own zeal for life and adventure. Before embracing her passion for storytelling, Tanya carved out a successful career in cyber security sales. However, the call of the written word proved irresistible, leading her to pursue writing full-time.

A keen sportswoman, Tanya has evented horses, competed in races ranging from 10km to ultra-marathons, and excelled as a triathlete. Her deep involvement in sports extends beyond personal achievement; she is also a dedicated volunteer, serving as a triathlon coach and parkrun Run Director. These experiences not only fuel her creativity but also infuse her writing with authenticity and vigour.

Tanya's narratives are as compelling and intricate as the paths she has run and raced. Her debut novel, "Men Are Like Buses," introduced readers to her wit and keen eye for human emotions. Her latest book, "Love and a Crocodile," continues to charm and engage, weaving humour and heartfelt moments into a tapestry of thrilling escapades and romantic dilemmas. Whether she's crafting stories or crossing finish lines, Tanya Knight celebrates the spirit of adventure that defines both her life and her novels.

Please find Tanya's website at
https://tanyaknightbooks.com
She has a Facebook page at "Tanya Knight Books"

Printed in Great Britain
by Amazon